CW00516341

# COLIN THE LIBRARIAN

# Colin THE LIBRARIAN

**Rich Parsons & Tony Keaveny**

Michael O'Mara Books Limited

This paperback edition first published in 1994 by
Michael O'Mara Books Limited
9 Lion Yard, Tremadoc Road
London SW4 7NQ

First published in Great Britain in 1993

Copyright © 1993 by Rich Parsons and Tony Keaveny

A CIP catalogue record for this book is available from
the British Library

ISBN 1-85479-952-5


Typeset by Florencetype Ltd, Kewstoke, Avon
Printed and bound in England by Cox & Wyman,
Reading

# Contents

# Prologue–The Creation

And yea! In the beginning was a rumble in the depths and there was light and dark and light again and lo! Threa was in flux. Then did Sylvester look down and behold! he did create from the molten rocks the gods who would shape the world to his exacting standards.

And yea! then did Sylvester fashion the monolith twins Yoof and Untilatelyoof whose combined responsibility was the vegetation. 'Go!' he boomed, 'and create trees, meadows, grass etc.'

And lo! were the twins confused having just that very minute been hewed from the very rock and being unfamiliar with any of these terms. Indeed, they did not yet even speak the language, as did not the other gods and lo! there was confusion and a certain number of mistakes in the early years.

And yea! did the twins take women folk from their nether regions and they were named Doezy and Bigdi. And to them was given the task, as soon as they could understand what was being said, of creating all the rodents, reptiles and crawly things as well as the insects, grobulets, throbulets and smelsigborgs.

(Editor's Note: this is not a mistake as throbulets

were indeed classified right from the beginning as being in the general category of creepy things. This was an error at the dawn of time and throbulets have been upset by it ever since.)

And yea! on the fourth day did Sylvester rest. But lo! having looked around he did find something was missing for did not the planet crawl with creepy and slithery things and more crawly things? But where was something bigger? And Sylvester intoned, 'Bigger, I need bigger!'

And did Sylvester make quadrupeds and sextupeds to a certain strictly controlled size and to them gave he the order, 'Keep the crawly population down.'

And yea! Sylvester rested once again and said, 'I'll tell you nothing about myself. That way no one can usurp me or create trouble for me.'

And yea! though he was wrong, yet Sylvester is remembered as the great one, the mighty one and the other one.

(*The Chronicles of Ancient Threa* Volume 1 Prologue)

# CHAPTER ONE

'Bow down before me, unworthy one, and pray
that I spare thine life, oh feeble and pathetic
creature. OK, I'll settle for another pint and a
packet of crisps, um, salt and vinegar please.'
Quoted from Sylvester's Thursday evening at the
Celestial Taverna, Cosmos Way.


'Art thou coming down for t'breakfast, Young 'un?'
His father's voice shocked Colin away from the
mirror. His morning ritual of deciding whether
the black spots on his face were hairs trying to push
through or just blackheads as he suspected, came to an
abrupt halt.

Damn! he thought. Twenty-one today and still no
need to shave. The wispy, down-like hairs protruding
from his chin still numbered only in their tens, and
showed no signs of multiplying, nor indeed of lengthening beyond the centimetre or so they had struggled
through so far.

'You don't have t'shout in my ear, father, you could
quite easily call from downstairs,' complained Colin,
continuing the daily conversation.

'What, and wake up t'neighbours?' boomed his
father.

Colin sighed and mentally noted that he would, definitely, start shaving today. He'd nip out from the
library at lunchtime and buy . . . um . . . a razor and
whatever else it was that he would need. He'd stun
them at FOCS tonight. They'd see him in a new light.

Wondering vaguely why he and his father went

through this same routine every morning, because he
never ate anything for breakfast anyway, Colin followed his father downstairs. He remembered that he
wasn't dressed, and wandered back upstairs to pull on
yesterday's shirt, his old school tie (lack of choice as
opposed to any sense of history) and his grey crimp-
lene trousers.

Slipping on his slip-ons and the battered tweed jacket, he looked again in the mirror. All five foot two of
him stared back; black hair speckled with dandruff all
over the place, spots erupting as he watched. Head
and Shoulders and Germolene were added to the
mental shopping list that had started with . . . um . . .
thingy. He couldn't decide whether he had the guts to
comb his hair in any particular way, so he left it sticking up at the back.

At the foot of the stairs a cup whistled past his head
and smashed against the wall.

'Sorry, lad, it slipped,' said his father, standing at the
sink six yards away.

Colin wondered why his father employed a
Yorkshire accent, having lived all his life in Clacton,
and why his mother was never home for breakfast. He
shut the door behind him and walked down the steps
to the street.

The walk to the Clacton Central Library and
Reference Centre was a short one and he arrived at 9.15
a.m on the dot as per usual. He mumbled hello to Ms
Jackster, smart and formidable as ever at the check-out
desk, and went to the back storeroom to shrug off his
jacket. He placed it, with a care absurd for such a battered object, on an unopened box of science fiction
periodicals destined for the reference section and then
ambled over to the desk to collect today's instructions.

'Re-file section 9;21;3A to book-dispensing agency C3;26 from 9A to 16C with alphanumeric sequence for customer appraisal,' read the carefully scripted note from Ms Jackster. He sighed at the thought of sorting out the crime and general catastrophe sections for what must be the fourth time in as many weeks; they all looked the same with those stupid yellow covers and foreign names all ending in 'z's.'

He reminded himself that the job was only temporary until he decided what to do with his life and that, after all, he was very lucky to have been promoted so quickly to Assistant Helper to the Librarian's Assistant just three years after leaving school with 10 O'levels and three failed A'levels in English, Latin and Greek. Colin brightened up with the thought that today, his twenty-first birthday, was the new beginning. He'd change his image. He'd start shaving, and do something about his hair.

Side parting.

No, central parting, just like was whatsisname, that chappie who did the quiz show on telly.

His stomach clenched as he thought about having to ask about the shaving stuff in the shop. What did he need? Razor blades, shaving cream, brush, a strap . . . or was it a strop? . . . anyway, all the stuff he remembered his dad mentioning in the past. He thought of the comments he would get from the Friends of the Conqueror Society (FOCS) meeting, and his stomach knotted. Maybe he'd leave it till next week. To console himself and calm down he sat in the chair and reached for a magazine.

His palm was moist as he eagerly flicked through the well thumbed pages of *National Geographic*, the shaving stress gone. He quickly found the pages that so often in the past he had turned to.

'What a pair of fun-bags!' he thought as he scrutinized the breasts of the big-boned warrior woman of the hidden tribe of the Amazon.

'I bet you don't get many of them to the pound,' he muttered aloud.

'Kilo,' said Ms Jackster, entering the room to find Colin.

'Pound, kilo, who gives a . . .' Colin broke off immediately. Panic set in and it was a good job that he had had the foresight to open a copy of Conan the Barbarian's latest epic on the desk, into which he quickly shoved the magazine. As he rushed past Ms Jackster in embarrassment he turned the corner and slipped the *National Geographic* on top of the Thriller Section. No one would find it there and he could retrieve it later.

As he worked through the day, Colin's mind drifted to that evening's meeting. The Friends of the Conqueror Society met every Saturday, and that was the focal point of his life. Based on *The Chronicles of Ancient Threa*, a three part fantasy novel or rather, collection of stories, about the fabulous planet Threa, its wonderful inhabitants, and its amazing history, it was something of a cult amongst many sci-fi buffs. Created by an unnamed writer or, perhaps writers, the hero of so many adventures was Krap the Conqueror, who battled, episode after episode, story after story, with the evil forces in various galaxies.

The Friends of the Conqueror Society (Clacton Branch) had been in existence for some time now, and every week the members met and role-played scenes and adventures from the saga. Colin had really felt at home in this world of fantasy and magic. He could be who he liked, do what he liked and he lived his life for those weekly meetings.

He was so entranced by Krap that he had memorised virtually all the books, studying them during free lessons at school, at home and in the library. In fact the prime reason why, three years ago, he had taken the job in the library was so that he could have unlimited access to the books and plenty of time to read and re-read them. It was also the reason he had failed his 'A' levels. He felt comfortable role-playing in Threa; more comfortable than being Colin. He had never had any friends, preferring to spend all his life in a dream world some light-years from Earth.

During his lunch-break, Colin walked purposefully out of the library and headed for Boots. As he looked for all the items on his list, he had the feeling that everyone was staring at him. The girls on the perfume counter were giggling, and he felt sure it was at him. How did they know? Other shoppers seemed to slow as they passed him, to check what he was buying? Then they'd hurry off to some other counter.

His basket remained empty. His face reddened and his spots erupted. He slunk off down to the food section to buy a sandwich. Anyway, he'd seen what he was going to buy (except for the strop, or strap) and maybe would come back later. Or he could borrow his dad's for a while. Yes, much better.

On his return he was taken to one side by Ms Jackster.

'Someone came in for you, Colin,' she whispered.

'Oh?' he mumbled, spitting crumbs of sandwich.

'I think he was from the, ahh, FUCK . . . ooh, excuse me, society or whatever it is you young things get up to,' she continued, undaunted.

Colin snapped to attention and forgot about brushing the tomato pips from his shirt and tie. Someone from FOCS! Looking for him! Maybe they DID like him after all! Maybe someone had remembered it was his birthday, or something crazy like that! Maybe they'd decided after five years of ignoring him he was OK and he wouldn't be bullied any more!

Well, not bullied exactly, but, you know, accepted more as an equal, sort of thing. It must have been his last role-play as Equution Arnoch that really made them realise!

Maybe it was Susan!

The love of his life (secretly) who had finally decided, perhaps, to go out with him! Even though he had never had the courage to ask her. And she was married. Oh well . . .

'Strange chap, about seven feet tall; two heads, brown cloak; You know, the type of stuff you people dress up in,' continued Ms Jackster in her loud stage whisper, as Colin glowed with new-found pride and self-confidence.

Now he could, and indeed should, go out and buy that shaving gear.

'Was it . . . was it Susan?' he enquired, hardly daring to mention her name and hardly thinking of his own reasoning behind the fact that it was very unlikely to have been her.

'Hardly, dear, she hasn't got two heads, has she? And I doubt that she is anything like seven feet tall! Oh, and we've decided to put you on the check-out on Monday now that you've come of age. Happy birthday!'

Colin grew impatient. Of course, the costumes were getting better all the time, and it was obviously someone dressed as a Tharg, Krap's arch enemies throughout the Chronicles, ready for tonight's meeting of FOCS . . . He didn't care about the check-out, though someone actually wishing him a happy birthday was quite a novelty.

'Who was it then?' he persisted.

'I don't know dear,' soothed Ms Jackster, slightly taken aback by his impatience. 'Anyway, I told him you'd be back later, so he said he would come back sometime. Well, not in so many words, but that was the impression he gave.'

Colin felt bitterly disappointed. The only time someone from FOCS had bothered to come and see him, and he'd missed it! Still he'd find out tonight.

The afternoon seemed to go on for ever. He couldn't concentrate on the crime section, and was more than once admonished by Ms Jackster in hushed tones for putting the authors out of sequence.

After what seemed like a lifetime 6 p.m. came. He grabbed his jacket and rushed out of the library. Feeling ten feet tall, he caught a bus to Princess Elizabeth Way, and arrived at the FOCS meeting early.

He entered the Grammar School pavilion where the meetings were held, and sat on a bench. He couldn't control his excitement waiting for everyone to arrive and tell him what they wanted him for. He fussed around, checking the metal table in the middle of the room; tightening the legs, though they did not need it, with the monkey wrench kept for that purpose. He sat back on the bench and just fingered the wrench for what seemed like hours and hours. When would they arrive?

First to turn up was Susan. She held a huge bunch of flowers. This was getting better and better! Colin leapt off the bench and shouted, 'Hi Susan!'

This was it!

'Oh, hello . . . um . . . thingy; what d'you think of the flowers?'

His heart soared.

'Oh, they're beautiful! Um, thanks . . .,' he spluttered.

'Yeah, I came through the park. Just for a lark I picked all the flowers,' continued Susan. 'They'll look good at home!'

Colin sank back into his seat. So it wasn't Susan. Come to think of it, she wasn't dressed as a Tharg, either. Damn!

The rest of the evening followed the same pattern. Every new arrival was greeted by Colin jumping up and shouting 'Hi!'.

Those that could be bothered to answer said hello and then huddled into their own little cliques, ignoring Colin entirely. The Hunt twins (Isaac and Eric), both dressed as Krap as usual, just punched Colin quite hard, as usual. Three Thargs arrived, none of whom admitted to wanting him for anything at all, and none of whom were seven feet tall, even in their make-up. Colin eventually left at about 8 p.m., shattered from the magic that had been dashed from his heart. He couldn't bring himself to join in the role-playing, even if the rest had let him. No one admitted to having called on him at the library. He was gutted.

As he walked home he tried to work off his depression by thinking of all the stuff he would buy tomorrow at Boots. Then they'd admit it. Then they'd treat him as a mate! Then they'd admit to secretly admiring him. Just wait!

He walked into the house in a trance. Mumbling goodnight to his parents, he wondered vaguely why his father seemed continually to be washing up, and why his mother always seemed to go out in the evenings alone. He went to bed. He may have cried a little, but didn't remember.

# CHAPTER TWO

'I said salt and vinegar, scumbag, not smokey
bacon!
Thou shouldst know that creative Gods touch
nothing that may be tainted with animal flesh!
Except pepperoni pizza. Extract of conversation at
the same Taverna on the same night.'

Colin sat back in his chair and placed the book on the desk in front of him. Krap the Conqueror had just completed another danger-riddled journey across the windswept, snow-covered, sinking-sanded jungles of the plant Threa; 2000 years after the ascendancy of the Tharg and no more than a cat's whisker away from Earth. Colin had been with him every step of the way.

As he watched the various members of the Clacton Central Library and Reference Centre file past his position to get their books stamped by the enormously plain Ms Jackster (whose lunch-break Colin was about to cover for the first time ever on the check-out desk, the day being Monday), he found inside himself a growing feeling of disgust at the subservience of the queue. Krap the Conqueror wouldn't queue! He was sure of that. Krap would toss his head, unsheath his broadsword and storm out of the building with the three (or more!) thrillers he had chosen, daring anyone to challenge him and stamp his books, cutting swathes through the pensioners and school-children in his way.

Colin felt sure that Krap would draw the line at carrying off Ms Jackster, even if it were physically

COLIN THE LIBRARIAN
*Entitled "Caught in the Act", this photo of Colin date-stamping books won third prize in Clacton Library's 'Mindless Git's Photography' competition, 1989.*

possible to move such a large mass; but woe betide any Shakira of the desert winds who happened upon the Clacton Central at that time! Her fate would be to be carried off on that mighty back to Krap's waterhouse in that far-distant and magical land . . . to fantastic adventures beyond the high street!

His dream over, Colin's gaze fell back to the line of people shuffling past with their chosen volumes to the dull, monotone thud of Ms Jackster's date stamp . . . a grey haired old woman of about ninety-seven clasping two Mills and Boon steamers; two children with *Enhanced Atlas of the World* (Colin had to admit that was a good choice); the Tharg with his *Chronicles of Ancient Threa* parts one and three; the elderly military type who . . . Colin started and almost fell off his chair.

A Tharg.

In his library. How had he missed the sight before? The twin-headed, four-armed traveller of the Cosmos, standing more than seven-feet tall in his brown all-encompassing cloak.

Four bright red eyes pierced Colin's brain in the first moments of thought control. This was no FOCS actor, this was for real. Was he the only one who had noticed the beast? Why didn't everyone panic or scream or run wildly from the library? For one ridiculous moment Colin thought the Tharg must be a regular library-goer, and so be a familiar sight, people just accepting his presence. Impossible! Pull yourself together! Thargs are NOT every-day inhabitants of Clacton or any other Earthly place come to that. And this was no role player.

As the red eyes burned further into his mind, gripping his brain in a vice-like embrace, Colin tried to move. He had to warn people . . . get them out of the way of this vile creation! He, after all, was one of the few people who knew the danger they presented, being an expert on *The Chronicles of Ancient Threa*, from those years of study and role-playing.

He vaguely heard Ms Jackster saying something about possibly being able to reserve part two of the Chronicles for the Tharg, and that it might take a week or so to come in, but the pain in his mind was reaching earthquake proportions as the eyes of the Tharg pierced his mind. At one point, the absurdity of being held by one head as the other discussed a book with his colleague bounced over his brain, but was forgotten as everything seemed to be squeezed out of his ears.

Suddenly the pain was gone; the hold released. The burning sensation disappeared. As his head collapsed forward onto the desk, it collided with that of the Tharg, sliced clean from the monster's shoulders with one mighty blow of a weapon. As the green blood, shooting skyward from the empty neck, fell in steaming showers upon him, Colin became aware of the blood-curdling scream that accompanied the blow. He looked up and, as the slime ran off his glasses, stared in awe at the rippling, sinewy muscles of the giant in front of him.

As Krap the Conqueror (Colin recognised him immediately) hacked at the lifeless form of the Tharg, Colin's brain was returning to some form of normality, released from the mind-hold in time to wonder at the sight of the sweat-laden fighting form in front of his counter. Krap was exactly as he had imagined: seven feet tall, almost the same wide, with not an ounce of fat on him, wearing just a loin cloth and metal frame glasses similar to the pair sported by Colin himself.

Every muscle was defined and taut as he carved the remains of the Tharg with his four-foot broadsword. The Killing Frenzy! thought Colin. Just as he had read in the sagas! Bloody Hell! he thought, what a perfect specimen! Everything a man should be!

'I'll just skin the bastard and make myself a new loin cloth because the stains will never come out of this one,' said Krap breathlessly to Colin, as the frenzy ended and Krap looked at the librarian, adjusting his glasses.

'You'll notice I have cut up the Tharg into thirty pieces, all perfectly matched, when skinned, to a treble thickness forty-eight inch-waist loin cloth pattern I have at home. Of course, the skin will take time to dry out, but it's the best in the home universe for keeping your cods warm!'

Colin gasped from the shock of the last three minutes; his mouth fell even wider open. Green gunge dribbled out. Krap the Conqueror not only acknowledged Colin's presence but was actually speaking to him as if they knew each other!

And he made his own loin cloths! Colin secretly kept his hand in at sewing items of ancient wear for the gatherings of the Friends of the Conqueror society but always claimed that his mother did it all. Yet here was Krap admitting; nay BOASTING even about his prowess with a needle and thread! Colin was lost in admiration for the huge man; a mighty killing machine with a penchant for needlework! Blimey!

Colin looked around as Krap got to work skinning the pieces of Tharg that lay strewn around the floor. The beast's blood was everywhere, still steaming-hot and oozing from the carcass. Remembering the pain, it was hard to feel any pity.

As Colin started to wipe his face and jacket with the back of his hand, he noticed Ms Jackster's body slumped next to him in her chair. The Tharg must have got to her before Krap could end its terrible life! Colin shuddered, frightened by his proximity to death, and the thought that it could have been him. Everyone had fled.

Krap looked up and saw the fear in Colin's face.

'Oh yes, sorry about your colleague, Colin, but I wasn't entirely sure at first which one was the Tharg,' he boomed. 'I thought I would take the uglier of the two first, but just as I saw the red blood spill, I noticed the two heads and four arms of the other, so I let him have it too. You've got to get up pretty early to catch me out but sometimes my glasses get a little steamed up and then it has to be first-come first severed!' Krap chuckled and Colin felt a strange sympathy for his problem. 'And your thriller section will need a little attention as I didn't have time to go round it.'

Colin could not honestly say he was too bothered about the demise of the gross Ms Jackster, but was astounded by the rest of the speech.

'How much damage did you do and how do you know my name and how did you get here? . . .' he mumbled to the giant who now rested on his sword, thirty flaps of Tharg skin hanging over one shoulder; green, oozing mess about his feet.

'About 7000 spondu worth; you will probably have to replace the entire shelving unit and then match the shade with the rest of the library,' responded Krap. 'As for the rest, well, you're special, Colin.'

Colin glowed at the compliment, but remained puzzled, wondering what the Conqueror could mean.

'You're one of the few that can reach across time and

galaxies with mental messages when the situation arises,' continued Krap. 'As soon as I picked up your thoughts about the Tharg, I sped through time and distance to your aid. Unfortunately my co-ordinates were slightly out and I materialized in your thriller section's bookcase, thus causing the damage. Anyway, your insurance should cover it.'

Colin nodded slowly, still not believing what was happening, but massively in awe of the super-hero who stood before him. And he had called him special. This guy was wonderful. Everything Colin had dreamed and more.

As Krap kicked the sloppy chunks of skinned Tharg into the reference section next door, he continued talking to Colin.

'So what did this bugger want with you? Must be something special to leap a couple of galaxies and a century or two. What did he say? I may as well tie up the loose ends as I'm here.'

'Umm . . . I'm not entirely sure,' said Colin slowly. 'He had two reference books on him at the desk and was asking about the missing third one . . . the second *Chronicle of Ancient Threa*, when you . . . er . . . killed him.'

Krap looked thunderstruck.

'*The Chronicles of Ancient Threa*,' he repeated slowly, 'parts one, two AND three?!'

'Yes . . . is it significant?' asked Colin, starting to feel a little more normal and useful.

'Quite apart from the fact that I only found two borrowing tickets on him, this Tharg must have been looking for clues in his race's quest for the vertebrae of Andrew the Spineless!' shouted Krap to no one in particular. 'I thought that they had given all that up a long time ago and accepted the end of their species, but they are obviously back on the trail!'

Colin knew the saga well . . . of Andrew, king of the Thargs and conqueror of Threa thousands of years ago, who had succumbed to a strange and baffling illness whilst on an expedition to a far-off planet. The surgeons at the Mayday Orbital Scientific Back-up Facility had started on an exploratory operation, but due to a mix-up on shift change-overs and subsequent misunderstandings, had extracted three vertebrae from each of his necks. When Andrew discovered the error, on coming out of the anaesthetic, his heads immediately tucked into the holes in his necks and he fell into a deep coma. Whether this was from pain or embarrassment nobody knew; meanwhile the vertebrae had been sold to Vincent the Grey, a visiting emperor and merchant, in exchange for the secret of eternal life.

Having ensured the survival of the species, sexual organs eventually disappeared from the Tharg's bodies through disuse; Thargs were sexless. However as the Chronicles explained, when Thargs started to die at the age of 3000–4000 years old, they realized that Vincent the Grey had duped them. He had extended their lives but not guaranteed them! Of course, by now, Vincent was long gone from the area; and so started the quest for the return of the vertebrae, in the hope that a transplant into the frozen body of Andrew the Spineless would revive the great and wise leader so that he could sort out the mess they had gotten themselves into: no eternal life and no reproductive organs.

Tharg battlecruisers and spies had been dispatched to all known galaxies, but with no sign of Vincent the Grey or the vertebrae. For a millenium the search continued, the Tharg race growing smaller and smaller until only a few million remained. They had retreated to a part of the planet Threa covered in bogs and marshes, there to eke out what remained of their pitiful lives, worshipping the still frozen body of Andrew the Spineless.

Until Now!

'I see you are of vast knowledge in the ancient stories!' boomed Krap suddenly.

Of course! All residents of Threa were capable of mind reading, although only some had the power of mind-control. As he had rushed through the substance of the Tharg saga, Krap must have followed his every thought. How embarrassing that could be. He would have to avoid all negative thought about the Mighty Conqueror.

'Too right, pal!' snorted the huge Krap, cleaning his broadsword. 'To complete your history, I have sworn that the brutal and disgusting tyranny of the Tharg empire shall never again rise to its former strength,' shouted Krap, his chest swelling to its mighty extent. 'Krap the Conqueror has chosen you, Colin the Librarian, as his friend and partner in this renewed race against the clock; the revival must be stopped! We must find the vertebrae of Andrew the Spineless and destroy them forever. We must find Vincent the Grey before the Thargs do. We must never allow a repeat of the Thargian monstrosities. Come, my friend, to the reference section and we shall plan our actions.'

The massive Krap, body still glistening with sweat, thumped the Chronicles down on the desk, splattering Colin, already seated, with green slime from the deceased Tharg.

'There must be a clue in here somewhere!' he

**KRAP THE CONQUEROR**
*The similarity between Krap's glasses and those of Colin
will be immediately apparent. It was rumoured that he wore
a wig, as most barbarians on Threa were blond. Anyway,
he's dead now, so it doesn't matter. Just goes to show,
though.*

thundered. 'The warlords would not risk sending someone to Earth unless they had done their homework.'

He looked at Colin as at a retarded child.

'It is a risk, Librarian, because innumerable of your diseases, so easily passed from one to the other, could wipe out the Tharg race; syphilis, NSU, thrush . . . that sort.'

Bugger the mind reading, thought Colin, there's little point in my even talking around here. His brain had only just registered the query about risks when the Conqueror had picked it up and explained. I don't suppose it's any use at all telling Krap that those sort of things are not common-or-garden flu-type viruses, he thought. Immediately he tried to cover the thought up with one of his favourite songs so as not to annoy the mighty warrior.

'What hills?' questioned Krap, staring rigidly at Colin. 'Can you show me the hills that live in song? That may be a clue!'

'No, no, sorry,' spluttered Colin, 'just a song to comfort me.'

The Conqueror slowly released Colin from his stare and turned back to the books.

'If you're going to screw around, I may just leave you to your fate at the hands of the Thargs, who obviously know of your knowledge,' he admonished.

'Sorry,' shuddered Colin, thinking of the four-armed, twin-headed beasts, 'it won't happen again.'

'Where is the part about Vincent the Grey in these books?' questioned Krap. 'That is our starting point.'

'Part one, chapter three, page 267,' stated Colin decisively. He knew these books backwards but could not think of any clues.

'There is no point in reading them backwards,' said Krap, still looking for page 267. 'Let us try by going in chronological order and in the correct sequence.'

Colin smothered the beginnings of a thought that this smug git was just showing off his mind reading skills and set himself to the task of finding the appropriate page for the Conqueror.

Krap took off his glasses and squinted at the book. He slowly read. 'Vincent the Grey. Chapter three. The Emperor's new teeth.'

Thirty minutes later Krap turned the page to 268. Colin was very frustrated at the slow plod of the Conqueror's reading, but felt it better to stick with it and let him get on with it, especially in view of the mind control the Conqueror could exercise and the broadsword tucked into his blood-stained loin-cloth.

Some forty minutes more elapsed before Krap grew tired of his task and read Colin's brain for the contents of the chapter; Colin, after all had read and re-read the Chronicles until he was word-perfect. His favourite role at the FOCS meetings was that of Krap, and he was well known for his knowledge of ancient Threa.

'So!' shouted Krap, springing to his feet, slipping over the remains of the Tharg and getting up off the floor rather sheepishly. 'Vincent the Grey was accompanied only by a band of nubile serving wenches and disappeared out towards Altar Major somewhere! Does he live forever?'

'It is said in the second Chronicles that he will thrive provided no one can out-argue him on the theories of sales and marketing strategy,' answered Colin. 'He believes a race can exist based on the ability to sell itself rather than procreate and has thus far managed to read every available book on the subject. He is so knowledgeable that the art of selling has become his form of reproduction. The nubile wenches were merely for pleasure and to be used as bargaining tools in his dealings with others. Every time he successfully sells the theory of the product he is strengthened.'

'Great Sylvesters,' exclaimed Krap, invoking the name of an ancient Threan prophet. 'What a horror story! Where is his race based?'

'All over the galaxy and beyond,' explained Colin, 'They're even here on Earth. They generally develop new ideas and try to sell them. That is why so many hard-sell items are discovered with such frequency and touted; for the survival of a species! It is interesting to note that the Grecians (the collective name for those of the race of Vincent the Grey)' . . . 'Yes, yes, I know' said Krap tersely . . . 'sell double-glazing, insurance, Amway products and water purifiers. Of course, many do not succeed and thus die pitifully, sapped of the strength and the will to go on but many more are successful and keep growing stronger and stronger. Once in a while Vincent himself starts a new pyramid to take strength from the masses, the sellers. I suppose he has the same form of operation in place all over the galaxy and the universe beyond.'

'The market traders of Threa!' exploded Krap. 'They too must be Grecians! I never realized!'

'More than likely,' said Colin eagerly, warming to his role as story teller. 'You see, Grecians take on the form of whatever race inhabits that particular planet or area. It is impossible to tell them apart from the natives except for the survival technique of constant harassment in pursuit of a sale.'

'So maybe we find one and torture him for the information,' said Krap darkly.

'No use, I'm afraid,' retorted Colin. 'They actually know nothing. Vincent is only known as "The Manager" or "The Boss" or "The Guvnor", and they refer to him as such. They only know that he exists, but never where he is. Vincent's greatest coup was the acquisition of the vertebrae and the power he thus gained, but beyond saying that a failed Grecian "has no backbone" or is "spineless", his underlings know little of the story, let alone the location of the bones.'

Krap looked despondent.

'Then what, Librarian, is our next move? I see no course of action here.'

'Well,' said Colin, leaning forward and adjusting his glasses, 'we could try the Mega-Corporation angle.' He felt a rush of excitement as he introduced his idea, first mooted at the 32nd FOCS convention only three months ago by none other than Colin himself.

'Go on,' said Krap impatiently. 'And who is the silken haired maiden you keep turning your thoughts to?'

Colin blushed; he hadn't realized before, but every time he thought of FOCS, he thought of Susan the Social Worker and his secret desire. He fantasized about carrying her away and brutally taking her in the manner of his hero Krap. He had, however, never done anything about it. He was sure she looked on him, if at all, as a bit of a wimp, and appeared to ignore him at every opportunity. Her husband, Bob, didn't attend the society's meetings, but it was rumoured that the occasional bruises and swellings she appeared with were the result of his beatings, caused by his excessive drinking and jealousy. It was just a rumour, but it had instilled in Colin a mortal hatred of Bob.

'Bob the Boozer? Wimp? Explain yourself,

Librarian!' yelled Krap, reading the trash floating through Colin's mind. 'No, on consideration, return to your idea for the tracing of Vincent the Grey. Time is of the essence.'

'Well,' continued Colin, his embarrassment fading to be replaced by an erection of excitement at his own idea, 'someone sets up a huge corporation, selling the purest form of marketing; ideas and concepts to businesses all over the Cosmos.'

'Like an advertising agency, you mean?' interrupted Krap, proud of his increasing knowledge of modern-day Earth (gleaned, as it happened, from Colin's brain).

'Yes, sort of, but without the morons that work in those places. Just two or three top people. The sales would be phenomenal, the potential strength quotient fantastic. It's odds-on that Vincent would hear about it. He would quickly realize that the operation would give him unbeatable strength and probably give him control of the entire universe!'

'But it is said that he is a tyrant as bad as Andrew the Spineless,' breathed Krap, 'and would his rule be any better than that of Thargs? I believe not.'

'Ah, but the beauty of my plan,' smarmed Colin, feeling for once superior, 'if you will let me finish, is that you create this business empire so quickly that you can base everything on loans from ordinary high street banks. Choose a bank like Lloyds, for example; mortgage yourself to the eyeballs; wait for the contact from Vincent; sign him on as a partner; go just a few pence overdrawn. The banks call in the loans, the business collapses and Vincent, who by now is dependent on the company, is lost. The strength quotient is lost, but you have Vincent.'

Krap was excited now and blurted, 'How long to set this up? Can we achieve it this afternoon, Librarian?'

Colin suddenly deflated to his five-foot two-inch pathetic self. Trust the Conqueror to pull out the one snag!

'It was calculated to take between two and three hundred years,' he mumbled.

'Too long, much too long,' spat Krap. 'We must search for another method. Come with me to Threa. There we shall contemplate the problem once more with the help of my trusted companions, Kelvin the Abbot and Bruce of the Ledger.'

The Conqueror picked up his thirty pieces of skinned Tharg, slung them over his shoulder, grabbed Colin by the arm and pushed him towards the door.

'This way, Colin the Librarian. We shall hasten to Threa. I with my broadsword and you with your knowledge; we shall surely win the day.'

Colin usually went through the reference library door but this time he went straight through the wall and fell head first into an oozing pool of fetid water, cold and slimy and filled with brown, tennis-ball sized globules. He panicked and thrashed about. Then he realized that the pool was no more than eighteen inches deep and he calmed down somewhat and got to his feet. The Conqueror was laughing, a huge belly-laugh, and stood next to him on a patch of dried mud.

'Sorry, oh Librarian, my coordinates were slightly out again. We should have arrived over there.' He pointed into the distance.

Colin was covered in cold gunge. He looked out over a flat, drab area of mud and stagnant pools such as the one he had materialized in. The smell was

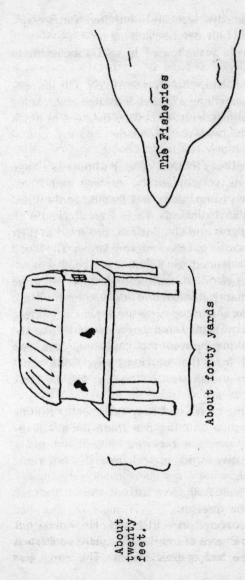

## KRAP'S WATERHOUSE

*The awesome size of this building can be measured by using the scales carefully provided by Colin. Being near the Fisheries of the Greenland, the name of the structure is believed to be derived from two Threan words; 'Water' which means a kind of liquid, and 'House' which denotes a sort of dwelling.*

The Fisheries

About forty yards

About twenty feet.

atrocious. He saw, some two hundred yards away, what he could only describe as a hut on stilts.

'THAT'S your waterhouse?' he said disbelieving to Krap.

'Yes,' replied Krap slightly defensively. 'Oh, it's only until I find something a bit better located and a tadge bigger. But at least nobody bothers me here, as much because of the smell as the isolation and my reputation.'

Colin had always thought of Krap's house as a huge marble palace, surrounded by gardens and lawns tended by his companions and leading to the great fisheries of the Greenlands. These were stocked with succulent fangras and stapilor fish, protected in their pens by the shoals of blood-sucking jarfish. The blood suckers were tended by Kelvin the Abbot, a mild-mannered ex-cleric of dark complexion; the more edible and marketable fangras and stapilor by Bruce of the Ledgers, a more aggressive person entirely, master of accountancy and purveyor of fish to the locality. Looking around the landscape, bare and brown apart from the occasional tree, Colin could appreciate why fish was the staple diet in these parts.

'I'm working on it,' said Krap impatiently, reading Colin's thoughts, 'but the fish trade doesn't really bring in too much in the way of cash nowadays, however creative Bruce is with his sales pitch and book-keeping.'

Colin suddenly flashed back to what Susan had been saying at the previous FOCS meeting. She had described this house perfectly based on her investigations into the Chronicles. He had disagreed with her as to the nature of Krap's dwelling but she, as usual, had ignored him. So she was right. Wait until he saw her again; she'd have to listen to him now!

Feeling a sharp pain in his leg, Colin looked down. He was still standing in the pool and one of the tennis balls had attached itself to his calf. It glowed red for a second, then doubled its size. He felt more pain and saw more tennis balls sliding up his legs and biting through the cloth of his trousers. He screamed, just as Krap skilfully detached the first of the balls with one deft flick of his broadsword. It fell back into the pool, oozing red pus.

'Jarfish,' explained Krap as he removed the rest. 'Blood suckers that have escaped from the pens. I shall have to speak to the Abbot about this later.'

Almost fainting at the sight of his own blood turning the water red, Colin scrambled out of the pool. Krap had stridden off to the house in the distance and Colin ran after him. He was whimpering slightly, but Krap ignored him.

As the pair approached the stilts supporting the house, Colin became more aware of the size of the building. Each of the four stilts was a tree trunk about three feet in diameter. These supported a platform about forty yards square, with a single-storeyed, mud-walled, thatched cottage on top. There was an area of about four feet of platform right around the house, serving as a balcony, or walkway. The platform itself was over twenty feet off the ground.

They reached the stilts and Krap threw Colin up onto the walkway. It hurt everywhere as he landed in a heap outside the huge front door. He was inspecting himself for broken bones when the Conqueror appeared over the edge, having shinned easily up one of the stilts, carrying his skins.

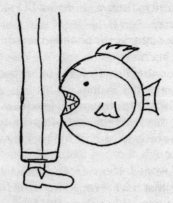

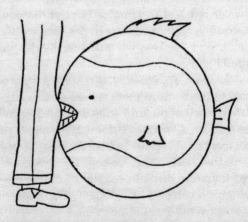

*Labelled 'BEFORE' and 'AFTER' these pictures show the blood-sucking JARFISH attached to Colin's leg.*
*It will be noted that, having sucked blood the jarfish almost doubles in size, swelled with the bounties of its feast of human plasma. Colin's leg, at the same time, remains about the same size.*

'Are you all right, Librarian?' asked Krap, obviously concerned. 'Only I meant to throw the skins up and carry you. Sorry.'

Krap flung open the door and entered, Colin close behind, rubbing his back.

'My God!' exclaimed Colin, 'you've been burgled. Look at the mess they've left.'

Indeed, tables were upturned, chairs smashed, and plates and glasses strewn everywhere. Rugs and furs were thrown on top of each other. Holes had been punched through the one-foot-thick mud walls and through the wooden floor. They let in the now dim light from outside. Fish were scattered on the floor and broken jugs littered the huge room.

'Don't worry, we'll get it cleared up soon,' responded Krap. 'We had a bit of a party here last night and I'm afraid things got a little silly. We all three drank too much; that's partly why I'm not too hot on my coordination today.'

Colin was suddenly overwhelmed by loneliness. Here he was, on a strange planet with, as his only friend, a barbarian with a hangover who skinned his enemies for clothes and held wild, house-wrecking parties. And the future of the universe rested squarely on his shoulders. He felt the urge to run, to get back to the library, to call the SAS and let them handle it; to ravage Susan and cling forever to her bosom. Krap read his concerns and slapped him heartily on the back.

'Fear not, Librarian,' he bellowed as Colin picked himself up from the base of the wall opposite. 'We shall win. Your brains and my tremendous strength and guile will ensure our victory. Then there will be time for the pleasure of coupling.'

A blood-curdling scream broke out from below the house. Colin's hair stood on end and he looked frantically around for somewhere to hide. Krap leapt fearlessly to the doorway, rushed out, tripped over the skins he had thrown down and fell head-first from the platform. Colin heard in this order: the Conqueror swear, then the full-throated roar of his battlecry, the unsheathing of the mighty sword and the squelch of flesh being sliced.

He crawled slowly to the door, not sure that it was a good idea, but compelled by the sound of fighting. As he peered cautiously over the platform edge, a huge spurt of green slime hit him in the face. He withdrew his head quickly, wiped his glasses on the drying pile of skins, and looked over again.

Krap the Conqueror, glistening with sweat, stood over the dead bodies of three Thargs. Six heads and various arms littered the area. Two other bodies, single heads attached, lay motionless a few feet away. Krap's sword shone green in the setting suns. He threw back his head and bellowed long and loud into the sky. The noise ended in a sob.

'They've killed Bruce of the Ledgers and Kelvin the Abbot,' he wailed. 'The bastards killed them. Why? Why? My life-long companions and trusted friends dead. Aaaaaahh!'

The final cry trailed off and Krap slowly moved to the two bodies dressed in shimmering blue cloaks of fish scales. He cradled each in turn, kissing the dead features, then laying the corpses gently back on the ground.

He looked up suddenly, a new resolve strengthening his stance.

'Colin the Librarian,' he boomed, 'we shall avenge

them. Let no stone remain unturned nor any planet stay in orbit until the wretched pig Grecian is found and the monster king of the Thargs destroyed.'

Colin tried to stop shaking at the sight before him. He shuffled slowly back into the house, still trying to come to terms with the events of the last few minutes, brushing off him the green blood of a Tharg and the brown mess of the pool as he went.

He thought pitifully to himself:

'Oh, shit.'

# CHAPTER THREE

'Time, gentlemen please!'
Snippet of conversation from the barman of the
Celestial Taverna, Cosmos Way.

B ut all was not well elsewhere in the universe. Untilatelyoof, one of the vegetable twins, had succumbed to a bout of the debilitating illness Duchelm disease. The other Gods, old and retired, had suddenly seen their chance to regain their power and have a bit of fun at the same time. They gradually eroded the power of the twins by increasing the size, numbers and strength of their own creations.

It was always the same, as Sylvester had so wisely said in the prologue, thought Yoof: any sign of weakness and the others went straight for the sap. It was the materialist in the power-hungry Gods coming out. He alone could not handle the situation, spending so much time nursing his ailing brother. Even their wives were empire-building at the expense of the vegetation. Slowly but surely the planet's vegetable life was dying at the hands of the other power-crazed Gods.

Gone were the days when the Yoof twins maintained the world's balance of power. It was so sad to see the bickering and bargaining going on around them. Soon the old gods would be walking the planet again. Besides incurring the wrath of Sylvester, mighty wars would erupt, disturbance unseen since before the beginning of time. The twins were forbidden to leave their home but how long would the rest of the gods obey! Indeed, it was so long since any of them had spoken to Sylvester (and even then they hadn't been able to understand him) that there were some who started to deny the continued life and vitality of the mightiest God of them all, He whose name is remembered.

Untilatelyoof stirred and called softly and weakly to his brother Yoof at the window.

'Lo, what noises of approaching gods do I hear?'

'Well,' responded Yoof, who was 126,392,234 years old and exactly the same age as his brother and only a few hours younger than a couple of the other gods, 'Pish passed a while ago quite quietly, not wishing his good woman stirred from her slumber. Oh, and Bigdi called to say she was leaving you.' He sat lightly on the edge of the bed, slowly rubbing his brother's brow. 'Then, er, Smellet and Thickun traipsed by more recently, I do believe intent on foul and evil doings,' he continued bitterly. 'For brother, ye have been asleep and poorly for some 4000 years.'

'Sylvester, 4000 years!' swore Untilatelyoof. 'How long be a year, brother, for have I never before heard the term? And what news of the vegetation?'

Yoof looked at his brother, who ailed in his bed still. His eyes were soft with tender thoughts.

'Alas, for 'tis all bad news, brother dearest. Creatures of the sea-Goddess have oozed poison all over our coral supremes, causing immense damage. You know, the ones we worked on together to celebrate our millionth creation since, er, creation.' His brother nodded weakly and closed his eyes. Yoof continued in a soft, low tone. 'Rats and mice have once again destroyed the crops in the fields. Our trees have been attacked with acid rain. I was unable to do anything without your help, brother dear, and the damage is significant. Vast areas of dessert are formed and oceans are barren.'

'You mean deserts, dear twin,' whispered Untilatelyoof from his bed.

Yoof, oblivious to the correction, cried out:

'Oh, yes, we have heroes; Krap does his very best as do others but the band is waning. Less and less do we see the Super-hero fighting for ecological balance on this once fair planet of ours!' Tears formed in his eyes. 'Get well soon, oh brother,' he implored. 'Be my strength and shield once more.'

'You know,' said Untilatelyoof, stirring again and raising himself to his elbows with no little effort. 'I feel better; the debilitating effect of the sickness seems to have eased.' He collapsed once more onto the bed. 'Just give me a few more centuries rest,' he begged as he dozed off once more into a fitful sleep.

Yoof, at his brother's side, soothed his forehead and then stroked his brother's.

'But who will help us while you regain your strength? For 'tis good news indeed that thee do better feel, but 'tis time needed that we have not got. Who is up to such a task?'

Untilatelyoof stirred for a third time. His eyes were still closed, but a look of grim determination came over his face, as if forcing his proud body to respond to the challenge of speaking once more.

'In my dream,' he mumbled, 'I saw one who is abroad this very moment. He is the chosen one. Find him, brother of mine, and bring him here so he may be briefed. For the love of all vegetable matter, and this planet, find him! Oh, shit . . .' The god fell into a deep sleep, his face showing lines of worry, as though experiencing a bad dream.

'Who could he mean?' wondered Yoof. 'Who on Threa could he . . .' YES. Shit! Surely that was it. Krap. He should get in touch with Krap, the mighty Conqueror.

There and then, the god scanned the universe in an attempt to contact the hairy-armed, rippling-muscled barbarian.

Sitting in Sidcup, the four pubescent teenagers were gathered to pit their wits against the assembled games consoles: Nintendo, Gameboy and Sega Masterdrive. Suddenly, the four spotty oiks were in a state of mind control from Yoof.

His mind probed their innermost secrets, and wondered why they thought of reproducing themselves every ten minutes or so. He was appalled at their memories of rubbing parts of their bodies whilst reading vile, base publications. What point could they possibly achieve besides a sore appendage and an aching wrist?

He sifted through their innermost thoughts and latched onto the reason for their meeting. He forgot the reason for the mind-relay process in the excitement.

'Got you, you bastards!' he sneered. He had found his goal; their reason for being was to pit their wits against those of a random number of computer-generated sequences. Whatever a computer was.

Suddenly Yoof realized that he had strayed out of range of the Conqueror and wasn't even on the same planet. He was in touch with mere, pathetic mortals elsewhere. He unlocked their minds. The teenagers hardly noticed.

Meanwhile Krap was skinning some unfortunate young . . . (Colin could not quite work out what it was that Krap was skinning). Anyway Krap was skinning it when he keeled over, mumbling something about a spikey-haired . . .

WHAM! Colin was in a state of mind control, his ethereal body shifted instantly to a land far, far away. He was on a different plane, and it wasn't Virgin!

An animal so strange approached Colin. It was an awesome sight, about eight feet high, hairy but garbed in a loin cloth that made Colin stare in disbelief.

'By the udder of another!' gasped Colin, suddenly speaking in rhyme.

The beast's mouth moved – Colin heard nothing. He just looked. The beast's garment was made from human skin . . . well, not just any skin, but from male reproductive organs; a dangle here and a dangle there – spherical here and there, and of all shapes and sizes.

'Jiminey Cricket, it looks like a wicket!' thought Colin (still thinking in rhyme, but getting annoyed at the inanities he was thinking).

Colin's ethereal body turned to run; he tripped and fell. The beast had a sword in his hand. Colin turned and watched in terror as the horrible thing approached. His attention was drawn to the sword, which was covered in mystic runes. Ornately carved, it looked like a piece of great workmanship.

'I bet that sword has seen some pink trombones,' he thought for no apparent reason, but glad that he was no longer thinking in rhyme.

A voice floated over. The beast's mouth was not moving. Colin suddenly realized that the beautiful singing voice emanated from the mystical, rune-covered sword.

The sword sung a song of a poof Geordie school master who once stood in the dense undergrowth.

'I've been stung!'

'Who are thee now?' was the mystical reply.

The ex-school teacher, now in a rune-covered sword, thought of the times he had penetrated a different kind of undergrowth with his weapon proudly held erect.

'Don't stand so close,' he yelled to Colin. 'The blade is sharp.'

The sword continued its woeful song in mellow tones.

'By the excrement of the Orals!' sang the teacher, 'How can Mother Nature be so put upon by mankind?' His voice trailed off and his thoughts went off at a tangent. Wondering what happened to Father Nature, the ex-superstar of stage, screen and mortarboard thought that maybe, after a night of bonking, Mother Nature ate Father Nature, like a praying mantis eats its mate.

Colin stumbled through the undergrowth, his breath quick, his pulse racing, his undergarments soiled, his temperature rising, his life-expectancy low. Running, running to escape the suicide-inducing lyrics of the mystically rune-covered sword.

'Friend or new Vauxhall five-door hatch-back?' barked the hideous creature, wielding the sword. It had recently been a computer-generated mammal projected onto a television screen in Sidcup.

Colin was reaching the end of his tether. He stood up, summoned up his last dregs of courage, puffed his chest, and spoke as manlily and gruffly as possible. He also put his best foot forward.

He screamed in pain.

'The bastard's trodden on me!' said the sword.

Yoof finally managed to break the spell and make

the dream disappear. He realised that his message to Krap had somehow entered the head of another, this Colin person. Part of a youth's mind from this place called Sidcup had also come along for the ride, and the combination had almost driven the receptor's mind completely mad. Yoof sat down to contemplate his failure.

# CHAPTER FOUR

'Your ten minute drinking up time has now well
expired. Would you please assist the barstaff and
finish your drinks immediately.'
Same person, 10 minutes later.

The following morning Krap and Colin finished
burying Bruce and Kelvin in the ground below the
house. As the sun broke clear over a desolate and
tree-less landscape, Colin watched Krap drag two
Tharg bodies over to the side of the pool at the far end
of the stilts and throw them in. A mass of brown tennis-ball jarfish seethed in their rush for the flesh and
Colin's legs started to ache and feel like jelly again,
remembering his experience in the pool. Krap climbed
back to the house. With a huge metal rod, he skewered
the remaining headless Tharg and set to making a fire.

'I think I know what's coming next, and I don't like
it,' thought Colin to himself; but also, of course, to
Krap.

'Fear not, Librarian!' snarled Krap, putting moss and
pieces of broken furniture on the fire. 'We grow strong
from our enemies. We eat the hatred with their bodies.
We feast today, for we have far to travel.'

Having thrown the Tharg on the fire, occasionally
returning to cook another side by grasping the red-hot
pole and heaving the body through forty-five degrees,
Krap busied himself by gathering up the heads and
limbs strewn about the area. With mighty heaves he

tossed them far out into the jarfish pool. Each splash was greeted with the same froth of bodies as the fish gorged themselves. Colin just sat a few yards from the fire, feeling sorry for himself and wondering how he would explain to FOCS that Krap's companions were no longer at his side, no longer tending the fish pens.

'How do you think this happened? I mean why? What did your compatriots know or do to anger the Thargs?' he questioned Krap.

'The Thargs must know of my quest,' spat Krap as he squatted near Colin and looked at the fire. 'They have sensed my purpose and came to destroy me.' He looked back sadly at the graves. 'Those poor fellows must have been returning from the pens when they met their doom. My heart cries for them.' He stood and shook a huge fist at the horizon, suddenly massive again; a new resolve coursing through his body. 'But my heart is strong. They shall have their revenge,' he yelled.

Colin, after his initial revulsion, found the Tharg flesh quite tasty, and munched his way through a roasted arm, carefully avoiding the boils and sores. Krap crammed large chunks into his mouth and spat out the bones.

'Come, Librarian, we leave this very morning for Kotestrent, on the borders of the Ion. There we may find our direction.'

Loin cloth stained green, sword dangling by his side, buttocks rippling, Krap strode off into the distance; Colin running along beside him. The fire spat Tharg fat and set alight Krap's waterhouse. Neither he nor Colin noticed.

Colin knew that the city of Kotestrent was some eighty Earth miles from Krap's place. The planet

Threa, according to the Chronicles, was about eight times the size of Earth, and one Threa mile was equivalent to ten Earth miles. Even if Colin tried to persuade himself that eight Threa miles really wasn't that far, he kept thinking of the Earth equivalent, and grew more and more tired as the walk went on. They had travelled barely an hour before he collapsed in a heap. Krap looked back.

'No time to lose, Librarian, get up and walk.'

'I can't,' breathed Colin, 'I'm tired out. And I think that one of my legs is gangrenous.' He looked at the pus oozing out of the jarfish wound, by now purple and black, and fell back in a faint.

He gradually came round, gingerly shaking, the fog from his head, and feeling sea-sick. Looking up, Colin found he was being carried by Krap in the manner of a baby, bouncing along in the mighty arms.

'Ah! Librarian! So you return to us,' bellowed Krap above his ear. 'I have poulticed your wound and will carry you to the village of Ors. There we shall find beasts to take us the rest of the way.'

The main sun was by now high, and Colin looked around in its glorious light. The scenery had magically changed from completely barren to what Colin imagined the Highlands of Scotland would look like. Huge, hitherto invisible mountains either side of the valley along which they trod (or rather Krap trod and he bounced). Still no vegetation; just grey rock and brown earth. Looking down at his leg, Colin saw what looked like mud caked onto the wound. It still oozed a little, but Colin really felt a lot better.

'I did think to leave your body and just take your head with me to reduce the weight, as that is all that seems to be of use,' bellowed Krap.

Colin looked up, startled, to see a smile flicker across the Conqueror's face. Thank God he's only joking, thought Colin; the relief quickly followed by mild anger at the mighty warrior's use of dry wit. Bloody comedian.

'Who is this god you are continually thanking, Librarian?' queried Krap.

'The equivalent of your Sylvester, I suppose,' replied Colin with little hesitation. 'An almighty, all-encompassing being, never seen but omnipresent to all believers.'

Krap grunted and walked on. Soon they arrived at the village of Ors, nestling in the mountains just above their valley path. Krap the Conqueror climbed the slope with ease and walked to the main street of the tiny iglooed village. The small, round houses of mud reminded Colin of beehives, covering an area no bigger than the library Colin worked in. There was no sign of life.

Krap unsheathed his sword, dropping Colin in the process. He raised the sword and screamed; 'I am Krap the Conqueror, afraid of neither man nor beast. I demand ye see me and respect me or feel my blade slice to thy gullets.'

There was not a single word in response, save the echo of Krap's scream. The place seemed deserted.

Krap advanced slowly into the village, sword held straight out in front. Glancing left, then right, then left, he waited on a knife edge for an attack.

Colin scrambled to his feet and started to run to catch up. Krap, startled by the sudden movement, yelled. He swung round and drove his blade at Colin. He pulled up short of Colin's frozen throat by about two millimetres.

'Librarian!' he shouted hoarsely.' You should know better. These hands are honed to the perfect death; trained to kill! No sudden movement or next time I may not be able to stop.' He adjusted his glasses and stalked petulantly off, to continue his search. Colin mumbled that he was s-s-s-sorry, and was about to move when a cold, putrid, webbed hand slapped itself moistly over his mouth. Another sneaked round his waist, one on his left arm, one on his right and one flopped up between his legs, crushing his testicles. He opened his mouth to scream in pain and terror. No sound came out. Instead he got a mouthful of flaky skin and pus from the hand over his mouth. As he was lifted effortlessly into the air he heard, somewhere far off, the Conqueror hissing: 'Be still, Librarian, I must concentrate! Just call if you see anything.'

'Bloody see anything?' screamed Colin in his mind as he came to rest. He was seven feet off the ground and two bright red eyes stared at him or, more precisely, through him. The eyes scanned his face from six inches away and hot, fetid breath passed in waves across his face.

Thrown to the ground, Colin twisted to see a line of twenty or thirty Thargs in bright green cloaks, each holding a pointed link of vertebrae. Each had one head collapsed and one erect. The Thargs stood between the journeying pair. Krap had read Colin's mind-scream and had turned to face the enemy who had appeared from nowhere. Krap's thoughts filled Colin's mind as the Conqueror levelled his sword at the centre of the line of Thargs. Berserkers?

'Yes,' shrieked Colin in the thought-transference conversation, 'Berserkers, elite Tharg troops thought

47

to have disappeared centuries ago. The SAS of the monster race.'

'SAS? What's SAS?' communicated Krap. 'Be precise and tell me all. I must know to defeat these creatures.'

Colin thought immediately and with surprising clarity for a man scared stupid, of page 379 of volume one of *The Chronicles of Ancient Threa*. Best to requote the Chronicles and give Krap the full picture. He visualized the page and read it in his mind (out loud in his mind, of course!).

'And yea, did Andrew mate, in frozen isolation and with little forethought or feeling, Olga, the daughter of Wendy, the facial-haired temptress from the frozen Northern wastes and daughter in turn of the Siberian Bladder Splatterer. The resultant multitude of demi-gods, using the copious, specially prepared quantities of brain-numbing, stomach-rumbling, flatulent, blarblingly-bottybluer liquid (incorporating, amongst secret ingredients, Monkey-discharge and own labelis), bred a super-race, strictly controlled and culled, to produce the elite – the stormtroopers. The maniacs loyal to the end to Andrew, reacted to the news of his likely non-recovery from the disastrous operation by tearing out their own spines with their bare hands. The squelching sounds echoed throughout the kingdom, for lo there were many. Jelly-fish-like objects were found in Berserker graveyards, putrefied and saddened by the apparent loss of their leader.

'It is fabled that Olga's sister Beverley, Goddess of Drenk and all things inebriate was wed to he that is known as the Durham Ox. She, taking after her moth-. er and being of great beauty and unparalleled bouncy chesty bits that were admired from afar, was capable of turning water into wine and wine into water (in due course). She took several Berserkers at youth and returned to her homeland in exile (with the great one whose name is never mentioned for fear of his wrath which is both terrible and great; also because it cannot be spoken by mortal tongue but was anyway called Mickey K), to develop the race still further and protect the Berserker species. They may be identified by their bright green cloaks that are but flaps of skin surrounding their bodies and so are in theory naked but far from embarrassed. It is further rumoured with or without just cause or foundation that they are at their most dangerous when flinging one spinal column at their foe; attempting to stab or throttle the enemy.

'Page 379.'

Colin concluded the description, verbatim, in about thirty seconds, and finished with his own words: 'Take care, Conqueror. Andrew the Spineless' stormtroopers are alive and dangerous.'

Krap's response was an ear-shattering scream, a lunge forward, and three beheaded Thargs. Blood (green) splattered all over Colin who was just behind them but he was getting used to all this now and simply wiped it away without the earlier revulsion. He saw Tharg spines whistling through the air towards Krap. They were sliced through with the broadsword and the rampant Thargs were slain. However, one Tharg caught the mighty man's left arm, ripping the bicep terribly, blood gushing red. He gasped, killed another Tharg, sliced another in-coming spine, and was hit by another spine on the thigh. Muscles tearing, sinews screaming and snapping, heads tumbling around him, innards spilling all over, Thargs dying and red blood mixing with green; it was an awesome sight.

Suddenly, a Berserker emerged from an igloo to one side, unseen by the wounded barbarian, ready to strike. Krap didn't see him, but Colin did. He screamed a warning and launched himself at the Tharg. He tripped over a prostrate corpse, smashed his head on a rock and dived into oblivion.

He came round, called weakly for his mother, rejected his erection for Susan, then remembered. He looked about, holding his aching head.

'Thee nearly had it, Earth-thing,' came a dull, monotonous voice. Colin looked at the nearest house, and recognized immediately the person who had spoken. Page 134, volume 2, Chronicles, he thought, in wonderment.

Wite Andrew of the Worth was sitting atop an igloo, finishing off a noose in grass strands; strong yet biodegradable and environmentally sound. A being so confused and despairing, that his body had developed to the degree that no sharp edges were to be found upon it. Thus it could inflict upon itself no mortal blow nor damage any dangly bits. In fact, it could not cease its incredibly monotonous existence.

'Thou must be terribly aggrieved to be still alive,' droned the Worth, walking over to test the bough of a tree that had conveniently appeared and to which he attached the noose.

Even Wite Andrew's death gurgle was somewhat boring, as Krap removed his head with a swish of his broadsword. Blood and sweat, bits of bone and muscle hanging out all over, the Conqueror stood for a moment, swaying gently as if in the wind, sword held aloft, and shrieked: 'Revenge is sweet, but not yet complete,' which Colin thought had a certain lyrical quality about it. Suddenly Krap spewed red and collapsed in a heap, amongst the thirty dead Thargs.

Colin looked at the heap of Krap, his own pain forgotten, and panic set in. If Krap were dead, as looked very much the case, so might Colin be. He would be stuck in another world, on another planet, with no friends, no help, and no return route to Earth. He wouldn't last long. Rushing over to the huge motionless form, Colin pulled Krap's head over to try and find the Conqueror's jugular pulse, as directed in the library's St John's Ambulance course. One mighty arm fell across and trapped Colin as he tried to turn the corpse over. He was crushed against the barbarian's mighty, if somewhat blood-stained chest. He struggled, but couldn't move out of the embrace. It took just twenty seconds for him to pass out.

As the haze cleared from his mind, Colin shook his head and immediately regretted it. His brain felt twice as big as his skull and was thumping fit to burst. He blinked in the sunlight and winced as he felt his ribs, bruised and battered, expanding with every breath. Suddenly he forgot his pain. His mouth fell open. There, in the bright sun was Krap, in six separate pieces, nailed to the side of one of the igloos. His limbs had been crudely hacked from his torso, as had been his head. The eyes were closed; the face almost serene in its lack of pain. Colin retched in fear and disgust at the scene in front of him. Questions replaced the pain whirling around in his head. Why? Who? How? The seemingly invincible Krap the Conqueror hung dead, cold, lifeless. Colin opened his mouth to scream: the only correct response to the events he had witnessed and the body on the igloo. Instead he threw up a stream of green bile from the depths of his stomach.

'Do reckon thee'll be needing food after that lot, yeay, Earthy!'

Colin spun round and saw, squatting on top of an igloo house, Wite Andrew of the Worth, soundlessly sharpening a cut-throat razor on a small stone.

'B-B-But you're dead,' stumbled Colin.

'Unfortunately not, oh Earthling of the reference library; oh yes, I know everything from your mind.

'I am condemned, as you know, to wander the reaches of Threa, far and wide, for time eternal, or until I cheer up. It's as boring as it sounds, you know.'

Wite Andrew's mind was a level drone buzzing into the corners of Colin's mind. Thinking back to page 134, volume 2 Colin recalled the description of Wite Andrew of the Worth. Here was a being so confused and despairing about life generally that its revenge upon the world it could never leave by normal means was to render opponents helpless by the use of speech and thought transference. Lulling the intended victim into a bored state of inactivity, slothfulness and finally complete and utter boredom, the target's vital functions started rapidly to slow until death set in.

'All that is true, barbarian. He that they called Krap the Conqueror tried to end my miserable life but unfortunately had no success,' recited Wite Andrew, pressing the razor blade first into his wrists. 'I live yet.' The razor sliced slowly into the skin but no blood appeared nor fell. Wite Andrew sighed heavily and continued slowly. 'I felt the urge for companionship, so I rescued you and hid you for a while, whilst the Berserkers returned in force to decorate that house.' He nodded over to Krap's tortured body.

Colin was dreadfully sad, but emotion was numbed as Wite Andrew droned on. 'I've not seen anything so moving since my days with the 'Disembowled Impalers'. I didn't much enjoy that either,' he mono-toned. Colin felt terribly depressed.

A loud, squelchy sound followed by several plops suddenly made Colin turn round. He was in time to see forty or more Tharg heads collapse as their spines were pulled out and held menacingly in front of them, all pointed at Colin. Behind these Berserkers were a dozen ordinary Thargs, surrounding one with . . . Colin choked and swallowed hard . . . three heads and a bright crimson cloak covering him from head to toe – a Commander General in full battle gear. A special hybrid whose combined three-headed intelligence had been developed in the old days to develop battle theo-ry and strategy to such effect that, in the days of the evil empire, nothing could match their attacks nor withstand their mighty, silent armies.

Voices had long ago become redundant to the Tharg, mind contact being by far the most convenient method of communication. Nobody but the Thargs knew whether they still had the ability to talk, but they cer-tainly chose not to.

There was something eerie about the silence sur-rounding Colin and Wite Andrew of the Worth but Colin's mind was a jumble of messages from the Thargs;

His mate killed Nobo!
Let's get him!
Little runt!
Spawn of a threawatchas!
Bastard of a Throbulet!

All minds laughed at this last one, a Throbulet being a tortoise-like amphibian with a single brain cell. It reproduced once every four thousand years, giving birth to one infant of increasingly lesser intelligence.

Several Thargs at this stage entered Wite Andrew's brain. The confusion of thoughts they encountered, so desperately despairing and depressing, caused three of their number to burst into tears before they could shut out the contact, pull out their second spines with a sad plop, and fall, jelly-like, into small personal pools on the ground.

Through the bewildering mass of mind-speak that ensued came a loud, clear message from the Commander General.

'I am Thong the Third, theoretician and Tharg extraordinaire, monster of mystery, suerat unstinting! I demand that you lay down your spine and return with us to our base at Kotestrent. There we shall investigate your usefulness and determine your fate.'

A low wailing moan came from Colin's left. 'Oh Sylvester, we're doomed! They're going to try and kill us!' said Wite Andrew in the closest he had ever come to excitement.

'Beware, unstable one,' came a message from Thong the Third, 'I am immune to your depression but my troops are not! Should any more fall victim to your negative vibrations, I shall be forced to deal with you immediately!'

Thong obviously did not know who Wite Andrew was. In macabre joke fashion, Wite Andrew entered the minds of three more inquisitive Tharg troopers who immediately popped their second spines and fell squelching to the ground.

'Go on then, end my life,' he challenged out loud.

Wite Andrew choked as one of the Thong's spines clattered around his neck and throttled him, choking the life-force out of him. When Wite Andrew's twitching had subsided, a Berserker retrieved the spine and took it back to thong, who slotted it back in to resume his full three-headed glory.

Wite Andrew of the Worth got to his feet amid a completely thunderstruck, awe-ridden audience. In a glory of mind-speak silence he quietly said, 'Oh, shit.'

It dawned on Thong; 'You must be Wite Andrew of the Worth; not even the Wall of Julian or the Bole of Shane are as effectively depressing nor as indestructible,' he gasped mentally.

Refinding his composure, he commanded all his troops to avoid Wite Andrew's mind, and said, 'We shall find a use for you, or else a way for you to die.'

'Good for the Thong,' came the reply.

It was difficult to know who was the most depressed on the trek to Kotestrent, Wite Andrew of the Worth with his tales of woe and desperation, disaster and gloom, or Colin who had to listen to them.

When Colin eventually keeled over, faint from hunger, they had been marching for barely four hours. The sun was still high but was starting to sink. Another rose and a third set.

# CHAPTER FIVE

'Haven't you got homes to go to? Oh, I see, well if
you're omnipresent then yes, I suppose you are
already at home. Just give me a few seconds to
figure this one out'
Same person, a few minutes later.

When he came to, he was lying on a bed of straw
in a dark, cellar-damp room. The only light
came from a candle on the far wall. In its flickering light he saw Wite Andrew of Worth hanging by
his ankles from two chains attached to the ceiling.

'W-what's happened?' asked Colin, trembling with
cold and fear.

'Oh, you collapsed, I carried you here and that's
about it,' answered Wite Andrew conveying more
boredom than was imaginable.

'But why are you hung like that?' Colin queried.

'Genetically or physically?' droned Wite Andrew,
straining his neck up against the forces of gravity to
see if anything had popped out of his loin-cloth. 'Oh,
yes, I see, well, one or two Berserkers disobeyed orders
and we got into a mind-lock together. They're dead
and I, unfortunately, am not. There's some food
there,' he nodded over to a wooden bowl with a red
slop in it.

Colin wolfed the gruel and the red lumps of gristly
meat in it.

'Not bad; better than Tharg! I wonder what it is?
Want some?'

'No thanks, I'm on hunger strike. Anyway, I'm not sure I could eat that Krap.'

Colin chuckled, then understood and threw up. He made do, eventually, with the loaf of bread left nearby.

By now he was desperate to go to the toilet. He'd wet himself just about every time he had become unconscious for one reason or another. His clothes stank, he stank, the cell stank, Wite Andrew stank, his vomit stank, and he felt bloody miserable.

'That's the spirit,' intoned Wite Andrew,'we'll get there yet.'

'I need to get out,' whinged Colin,'I must get home. I don't like it here any more. I'm so depressed, I can't stand it.'

At that moment the cell door swung ajar and Colin turned round at the squeaking. Through the door came the most gorgeous woman Colin had ever seen. More stunning and captivating than Susan the Social Worker, he thought! She wore a belly-dancer's bikini which did nothing to hide her voluptuous figure. Her long dark hair reached her waist and her full, pouting lips seemed to quiver as if in anticipation. Colin stood up, but she glided past him and over to where Wite Andrew hung. She ran her hands silently up and down his inverted body; squeezing, moulding and touching. Wite Andrew yawned.

'Maybe I'll die of gonorrhoea or syphilis yet, eh?' he monotoned, apparently untroubled by the attention, though Colin thought he caught a slight uplift of the voice towards the end of the sentence.

The girl stepped away, took off her bikini top and in the same movement squatted down and pushed each large, firm breast into Wite Andrew's face. Colin's erection by now was matched only by that of Wite Andrew's.

The girl stood, stripped completely, clamped Wite Andrew's head between her thighs and started to peel off his loin-cloth. Colin barely had time to notice the rise in Andrew's voice before he himself ejaculated.

'Oh, Sylvester. What is this?' moaned Wite Andrew, two octaves higher than usual. He started to whine, then shout, then scream. As the scream grew, the girl blew, and Wite Andrew of the Worth's head exploded. Colin, covered in bits of brain and splashes of blood that were a very boring brown in colour suddenly marvelled at the ingenuity of the Thargs. They had killed Wite Andrew of the Worth at long last, with a surfeit of pleasure, the like of which he had never previously encountered. It had reacted against his depression, overloaded him and finally killed him.

As the girl turned, Colin wondered if he was next, sure that he would also die and questioning whether he minded or not. But she strode past him with a worried expression on her face and left the cell.

Colin suddenly realized that the door to the cell was still open. Moving rather gingerly due to the mess he had made in his trousers, he looked out. No one was about so he moved out into the corridor, breath held to catch any sounds, loins sticky and wet and really rather uncomfortable. Forty yards on, he arrived back at his cell from the same direction in which he had left it. How, he did not know, but anyway took the opposite direction.

Some hundred yards on he heard a mumble of voices, with one in particular raised to a shout. He pressed his ear to the door that appeared at the end of the corridor.

'You stupid tart, by all that's Kotler! It was the other one you were supposed to screw, not the bloody manic depressive. Sylvester! If I had the tits I'd do it myself! Now go and sleep with the Thargs and *don't* mess up again!'

Colin fell through the doorway as the girl he had seen earlier pulled the door open and rushed through into the corridor, wailing (presumably at her punishment) and naked as when she had left the cell.

'Oh yes, and what do you want, Blovestichst?' asked a voice uncomfortably similar to that of Krap the deceased Conqueror. Colin looked up to see he was in a huge hall. Timber beams went off in all directions across the ceiling; stone floor and high, thatched roof. Candles burned everywhere casting a flickering, eerie light and giving out the same smell as in the corridor only stronger, more pungent.

There were six people in the room; four were beautiful females, almost exact replicas of the one that had just rushed past Colin. Another was instantly recognizable as Thong the Third, Tharg Commander General in his splendid, shimmering cloak. All three heads were erect and proud. Six red eyes pierced Colin's head with their steel-like stare.

Colin looked at the sixth person and gasped. He lay on a bed of sorts to the right of Thong, and surrounded by the four beautiful maidens. The face forced Colin's mind to leap immediately to page 729, volume 1 of *The Chronicles of Ancient Threa.*

'And there did rise the mighty form of Vincent the Grey, he with no bodily hair darker in shade than the snow. A terrible, wizened figure that somehow emanated inner strength, the resolve to sell; the perfection of marketing; physically wretched but outstandingly there; the overall leader; the boss; the manager; the king of all that is sold in idea and theory, ideologies and hard-sell. And thus did Vincent the Grey build and swell to his full demonic height and fitness. And so does he waver and change endlessly until such time as he doesn't. And the mind-speak was beyond him, yet the spoken word his weapon and the rubbery bits were bouncy.'

That is correct, Librarian, sneered Tharg into his mind. Yes, Colin of the lost cause, it is indeed Vincent the Grey of the rubbery bits, master of the purchase pattern and buyer behaviour!

'Come on, spit it out, what do you want?' gushed Vincent to Colin.'Time is money, money is success, success is strength, strength is pleasure, and I have *not* got all reya!' (a reference to the Grecian year, some four times the length of one on Earth, Colin knew).

The girls, all dressed as slave girls, shifted uncomfortably around their master, as Colin opened his mouth to speak. But fear gripped his throat and held it closed. A strangled bleep was all that escaped.

'Look, Librarian, for I know 'tis you, let's keep it simple,' said Vincent the Grey as he got unsteadily up onto his feet helped by the nubile serving wenches.

Aye, communicated Thong to Colin, he is sapped of strength and has sold nothing for months. We keep him stimulated physically and he slowly forgets his art. He will soon be ours and will reveal the whereabouts of the vertebrae of Andrew the Spineless. Then we shall dispose of him. And he can't read our intentions through our minds. He has no mind communication.

Colin almost added to the mess in his trousers. He had found Vincent the Grey. And the Thargs had him.

He got to his feet and stared wildly around him. There were no doors to the vast hall save that through which he had fallen. But that went nowhere. He had followed both directions and found only the one door. What the hell was going on?

'What's up, Librarian, looking at the candles? They're pretty Krap, aren't they?' said Vincent, approaching Colin slowly and carefully.

Colin started to say that, actually they were quite nice, then understood and threw up over the advancing Vincent. They'd melted his friend down and used the body-fat to make candles. That was the sickly-sweet smell he had noticed previously. Burning Krap. He retched again. Vincent moved quickly left but still got caught by the sputum from Colin's bowel upheaval.

'Sylvester!' yelled Vincent as he brushed down his yellow cloak rather weakly.'You get a super idea: sell candles to the Thargs and what happens? Bile all over, that's what.'

Never mind the old one's rantings, thought Thong to Colin, you will die soon enough. We cannot let you tell the Grey one of our plans.

Vincent now had a hold on Colin. His hands were on Colin's shoulders and he pushed the librarian back against the wall. He followed and placed his hands squarely on Colin's thighs.

'Fancy a little stimulation, my beauty?' leered Vincent, face pushed into Colin's.'It'll cost you, you know. Let's haggle.'

Colin felt awfully sick again at this new turn of events, then Vincent whispered,'Shut up and listen. Vertebrae: two by three, in your pocket. Just put them there . . . I am finished . . . Can't sell a fucking thing here . . . you must dispose . . . don't argue, Librarian, the galaxy depends on you. Now open your mouth.'

Colin automatically did as he was told, and Vincent stuck his tongue into the Librarian's throat, caressing his tonsils, lips meeting. Colin's automatic reaction was to clamp his jaws shut and close his eyes. He opened them and felt Vincent's tongue still in his mouth; Vincent, however was four yards away, blood gushing from his mouth, screaming and crying. Colin spat out the tongue and retched; nothing came.

Vincent lay on the floor screaming. The girls, eyes wide in alarm, lay spell-bound on the bed, and Thong hurried over to the mess. Enough, Librarian, he screamed at Colin's mind. We need him at present. Desist, do not destroy him, oh brave one.

Colin was so confused that Vincent's words had not yet registered and so had not been passed on to the mind-reading Thong. As the Tharg dragged Vincent out of the door, Colin remembered and put his hand into his wet, foul-smelling trouser pocket. There he found two chains of small, hard bones. His mind screamed: Andrew the Spineless's vertebrae. He didn't want them . . . what was he to do? He adopted the foetal position on the floor and sucked his thumb furiously. Little solace. Still the situation, still the problem. His mind thumped and his head ached. 'Not again!' he thought as he slid down the ramp into unconsciousness.

# CHAPTER SIX

'Look, I'm knackered. I'm off home. Help your-
selves if you want anything else and leave the
money in the till.'
Defeated barman at the Celestial Taverna, Cosmos
Way, very early Friday morning.

Yoof was furious. The dream had failed to stir the
mighty Krap. Could it possibly be that the fire of
life no longer burned in the loins of the mighty
man?

But who was this Librarian chappie? He had had a
brief, fleeting image of one called Colin the Librarian,
or something like that, of hills that sang and of worry
and anxiety, of great stress. Could it be that this was a
man undertaking a great task?

Well, thought Yoof, if he is, or anyway was, in the
company of the mighty Krap then he must be of that
Ilk, stressed or not. But how to reach this super-hero?
The dream had not moved him, probably due to the
confusion already reigning in his head. Stress concen-
trated a mind wonderfully to the extent that other
things were often ignored.

Just then two horsegod things ambled past the window, a bale of hay held aloft: Of course; the Centaurs.
These creatures half man, half animal, were the first
creatures to have been given life in the early days.
Unfortunately, after a particularly wild party to celebrate the invention of the Fjord (or 'Crimped coastal
feature' in God-speak or 'Damn, I didn't mean to cut

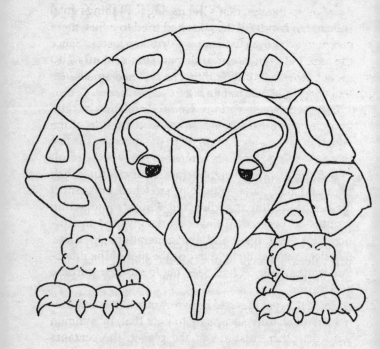

**PORTRAIT OF THROBULET**
*Drawn by Wealthy Vicars.*
*A very slow and very rare creature, throbulet matings are almost unheard of. A solitary animal, multiple orgasms are few and far between.*
*The gestation period is about two hundred years, though no-one has ever waited around to find out accurately.*
*It reminds Colin of a cross between a tortoise and something else that he's never quite managed to put his finger on, though he feels like it should be on the tip of his tongue sometimes.*

66

that bit out. These damned celestial scissors are crap . . . wait up though, that's interesting . . .') things got a little out of hand. All the gods had tried to adjust these creations according to their own drunken tastes. Hence the mix between horse and man (the centaurs also grew bushes out of their buttocks and had small, useless wings and a dorsal fin).

Battles between various Gods, drunken and giggling, to create something of use to their side of the equation of life raged all night. In the morning the last thing the hungover Gods wanted to see was the result of their petulance the night before. Four creatures, half man and half horse with long stretched tails, small bushes protruding, tiny fins and wings, squidged up mouths all covered in finger-marks awaited instructions for their lives and the generations to come. Smellet banished them to live at the foot of the mountain until a decision had been made on their purpose and future.

There the centaurs had been forgotten. (It is interesting though hardly surprising to note that, in common with the other creatures of the planet, the centaurs were now completely unaware of the presence of the gods. Consequently when bales of hay tumbled from the sky now and again, they were greeted with 'Look out, there's another one!' and 'Will you fuck off, whoever you are!' Especially after one of the centaurs was stunned when a bale of hay caught it unawares.) Anyway, as the centaurs were definitely not fish or vegetation or birds they were left alone by the gods to continue their miserable existences.

But now, thought Yoof triumphantly, although I cannot undo that which is done, I could give them a little heaven of their own to live in. Nice lawn pastures, small green bushes bursting with juicy leaves, dande-lions by the score and burdocks as well. (His mouth started to water.) H'm, that would be nice. He could do nothing to keep the centaur race going since, at the time of their creation, the gods knew nothing about sexual organs. Procreation to them was handfuls of earth or rock or DNA or other biological explosions. As a result, the four centaurs were sexless, but he could make their endless, lonely years more bearable.

Now, how to contact them? Yoof had no hay to throw and couldn't really write the centaurs a note, never having had the need to learn to write being a god.

Of course, use his own creations: the grass and the trees. Contact them that way. The creatures were sur-rounded by vegetation; they were sure to notice. He sprang to the window, and whistled up the nearest bush. He started to tickle its root systems.

'Send the signal,' he mentally transmitted to it. 'Rustle leaves, and speak to these creatures at the foot of the mountain! Call them here! Do your stuff vegeta-tion; relay my thoughts! Bring them here, *now*.'

The leaves started to rustle, though there was no wind. A Mexican wave of vegetation carried down the mountainside. 'Soon,' thought Yoof, 'soon they will be here.'

The message reached the bushes and the grass in the valley. Plants swayed hypnotically and flowers gyrated, giving sound to the thoughts so urgently transmitted moments earlier. Trees moved, though there was no wind. The four centaurs, hideous mouths feeding hungrily on the grass, looked up as one.

'What's going on, neigh whinney?' contorted the one who was called Thade, his puckered lips straining to voice his thoughts in a low, depressed manner. He watched the movement with interest.

'Dunno, neigh, almost squersh as if, whinney, they're trying, neigh, to whoosh tell us something,' said Raw aggressively, as they congregated around the vegetation that swayed and rustled, whispering insistently at them.

'Bloody, whinney, strange that,' neighed Mefani hungrily, head rocking as it followed the motion of the plants.

'Weird, neigh, like those whinney brrrr bloody neigh flying whersh bales of neigh hay,' agreed Eclipsnet, as the sores erupted on his flank forcing him into silence.

The bush was gearing itself up finally to give the message to its captivated audience when the four horse men of the puckered lips ate it. They then returned to their grazing, ignoring the insistent, whispered pleas of the remaining flora and fauna about them.

# CHAPTER SEVEN

'Before thou leavest, oh mortal servant to the
Gods, thou shalt answer to me, Sylvester,
omnipresent one and creator of worlds!'
Sylvester, omnipresent God, whilst at Celestial
Taverna, Cosmos Way, early Friday morning,
rather the worse for wear.

Trying to move the fifty tonne weight that felt as
though it were crushing his head, Colin slowly
opened his eyes. He was being comforted by
someone, someone familiar.

'There, there, Colin, you must have fallen asleep! It's
your shift now.' He looked up to see Ms Jackster; one
arm behind his head supported him while the other
smoothed his hair slowly, almost lovingly.

'Oh, thank God, Ms Jackster. I've just had the most
awful nightmare. Oh, I'm so glad to see you. I thought
you were dead. I mean that Krap had . . . and then I
went, and he got . . . and the Thargs . . . and . . . my
God.'

A sudden and immense wave of relief washed over
him. The dream had seemed so real, so life-like. He
could even still smell the horrible odour of his several-
times-fouled trousers.

Ms Jackster smiled at him, a smile that spread half
way around her face and then grew to envelop her
entire head. The huge mouth opened and spewed hot,
fetid liquid all over him. The image swam, and then
faded, to be replaced by the face of Vincent the Grey.

Colin was confused . . . then his relief ended.

Everything that had happened hadn't been a dream. Ms Jackster was the dream. He screamed but no sound came. He tried to get up, but couldn't. He started to cry, closed his eyes to shut out the fear, then reopened them.

'Huh uh, Hirarian, oo hood ow eeta,' scolded Vincent, tonguelessly.

'Where am I?' asked Colin, still sobbing.

'Uooh hainged wiv me in ve gungon, aitin fuh exhecuton.'

Vincent spoke with some difficulty. Little specs of blood still spat from his mouth.

Colin noticed a pain in his feet. Then realised that both he and Vincent were chained upside down in the dungeon as had only Wite Andrew of the Worth been some few hours . . . days? . . . months? . . . minutes . . . before. The weight on Colin's head was a combination of the blood and gravity (and, of course, the ever increasing soft spot).

'Herhebray,' spat Vincent.

'What?'

'Herhebray!' he repeated in a fresh shower of blood that covered Colin's face, making him feel sick.

'What?' he spluttered

'Huddy hukin herhebray!' cried Vincent furiously.

'Oh, oh the vertebrae . . . yes . . . yes, I have them.' Colin felt the shapes secure in his upside down pocket.

Just then an explosion ripped through the cell. Colin was flung twenty or thirty metres away by the force of the blast. He was hit in the stomach by Vincent's head, then his legs, then one of his arms. He guessed Vincent was dead.

As he picked himself up from the shattered remains of the wall from which he had been hanging, he saw a shape loom through the dust that still floated in the air.

'Colin? Colin the Librarian?'

Colin nodded stiffly, unable to speak.

'Quick! This way. No time to lose!'

Colin was dragged off, but jerked to a halt by his ankles that were still chained to a huge chunk of wall that now lay on the floor. The arms that grabbed him, pulled his torso with greater and greater strength until something gave. He hoped it wasn't his ankles but, having stopped screaming, found it to have been the manacles. He was rushed through corridor after corridor, never quite seeing who lead him, but pleased to have found a friend. Or at least someone concerned for his welfare.

They halted at a huge oak door and Colin, while trying to get his breath back, took stock of his rescuer. He suddenly shuddered. Page 429, volume 3, the Chronicles.

'And one did come, so swift, so strong, that the ancient rulers were almost powerless to resist the force. The body wiggling, primeval movement of the bronzed, oil-skinned, taut-nippled marauder was ever in evidence in times of crisis. And so the Nels of Paulon did spread good and kind deeds to all, until captured by the Tharg leader Tango, who imprisoned him by setting the trap of blows. There, condemned to an eternal life of agony, it is rumoured that he shall rise but once, and once only in the time of crying and the wailing skies. And the good be bad and the ugly magnificent! His face a thousand writhing corpses, his body a mass of bloodied flesh, he shall reform and be strong once more. But mark ye, once and once only!'

'You're Nels of the Paulon, aren't you?' shrieked Colin.

'Yes, yes, not now,' admonished Nels, preparing to open the door.

'But I thought your face was a thousand writhing corpses, and . . .'

'Listen, I'm just back this once, and if we can pull it off we're in clover, and anyway it's only in my imprisonment that my face . . . oh, never mind!' At this point Nels barged the door open.

'Pull what off, the door?' asked Colin stupidly, as he followed Nels into the bright sunshine.

Nels of the Paulon stopped and turned. They were in a vast green meadow, stretching as far as the eye could see, dotted with wild red flowers.

'We must get the vertebrae of Andrew the Spineless to Mike Thom; the only person who can grind them to dust and dispose of them . . . It is our only hope to rid the planet, the universe and whatever is bigger than that of the dreaded Tharg empire, part two. Don't you know the Chronicles?'

'Yes, yes, I do, but not that bit, I've never read it,' puzzled Colin.

'Page something or other, volume four, *Chronicles of* . . .' said Nels vaguely, searching for something on the horizon.

'Volume four? There's a volume four?' Colin felt even more defenceless at his lack of knowledge, but all the same exhilarated at the prospect of a previously unknown volume four of the ancient writings.

'Not yet, we're in the middle of it. We're creating it,' said Nels, lining up the sun with a point in the distance.

Colin suddenly felt the warm sun on his back, and revelled in the astonishing knowledge of his participation in the creation of history on the planet Threa. How wonderful. FOCS would soon be reading of the exploits of Colin the Librarian and his quest to save the universe. If he did.

He suddenly deflated. How the hell was he to do it? Mike Thom, the 'invisible'. There one minute, gone the next. It all seemed too hopeless. He turned to Nels of the Paulon to voice his doubts and maybe receive some comfort.

'Fear not, Librarian, we shall win. We *have* to win; we must find the grinder!'

Colin looked back at the door they had just come through and felt no surprise to see it had disappeared. They stood together in the vast meadow, not a tree in sight. He was getting used to this by now.

'How did you know where I was?' he asked of Nels as they started to make their way towards the town that started to appear on the horizon.

'I am, and always have been, telepathically in tune to the Vertebrae of Andrew the Spineless,' Nels explained. 'You will note that I am separated by two volumes and several hundred years of history from their removal. However, during my do-gooding, it became evident to me that, should I only be given one short escape to save this planet and others and the big thing that they're all in, it should be attached to, and triggered by, the one most dangerous scenario in the history, past or present, of this or any other world. I managed to meet with Vincent the Grey years ago, and persuaded him to let me touch the vertebrae while he was trying to interest me in buying a flueless gas fire with synthetic stone surround. That was the link established; when Tango incarcerated me soon thereafter, the one thing that would free me would be the reactivation of this issue created by the bones changing hands.'

'But why now? How did you know?' asked Colin, not realizing that the question had already been answered.

Vincent decided to embellish a little.

'I looked in the fires of the ever burning crystal pigskin monetula in the polygon of enormous wardrobed chandelier fliers, and felt that the vertebrae had changed hands.' Actually, he had heard it in an incarceration bar, where all those incarcerated could get a beer while they were waiting to be released.

'This was something I had hoped would never happen. While they were with Vincent the Grey, lord of all that sells, they were safe, never to be dislodged, fixed by the strength exerted by his greed for power and strength. He would never relinquish possession, because the highest bid would never satisfy him. He would want to sell for more. Haggle and bargain. So I had to find out what had happened. I blew the cell, and here I am!'

'But why should Vincent give me the vertebrae? He is surely invincible unless he cannot sell or contact . . .' Colin trailed off thoughtfully as he wiped the animal dung from his shoes that he had recently stepped in (the dung, not the shoes, added Nels for the record).

'Yes, the Thargs had brilliantly lured him into a trap; no chance of selling anything, and no doors to the outside to entertain salesmen from whom he could gain strength. He was slowly dying anyway. Mind you, biting his tongue off did nothing to help, I'll admit. He realized this and gave you the vertebrae to avoid a Tharg success.'

'But why didn't they just take the vertebrae from him?'

'They were playing with his life; they wanted him dead and had time to wait. When he was dead they would take the bones from him. What's a few days when you've waited centuries?'

Nels stopped walking and turned to Colin, his sinewy body glistening with sweat, every muscle defined, every vein apparent.

'But I'm so glad he gave them to you, Librarian,' he said softly, bending down to kiss Colin full on the lips.

Colin spat. 'Oh shit! You're a poof.'

'You reject me, Librarian? I have not pleased you?' Nels sounded hurt, and pouted to emphasise the effect. 'Do you not crave for the twinning of our bodies? For the mixing of our sweat as we tumble lazily around in tender loveplay? Do your loins not ache to be astride me, riding . . . until we are both collapsing to the floor, spent from many hours of exploring each other's bits and areas?'

'Fuck off!' shouted Colin, scared now that the lean, muscular champion of the underbodies had a canoe in his loin-cloth, or at the very least a banana, or a . . . no, no, he couldn't face it! Having used only his fourth swear-word of the entire adventure, Colin suddenly saw red. To be dashed from hope to fear in three short sentences was just too much! He grasped Nels by the arms, jumped up like he'd seen in the films and, with a grunt of effort, butted Nels of the Paulon full in the face.

When he regained consciousness, Colin found himself lying on the bank of a small river. He saw his clothes laid out on stones in the sunshine and felt a cold dampness over his nose, through which he couldn't breathe. He felt blocked-up and unhappy.

Nels of the Paulon bent over him and dabbed at his

nose with moist leaves. He jumped. No clothes, his mind told him, Nels still there, him out cold. Oh God, he'd been violated! He clenched his buttocks, as if expecting to find something still there.

'No, no, Librarian, do not worry,' giggled Nels gaily, reading his anxious mind. 'I have merely washed your clothes as they smelt horrible! That's quite a self-defence mechanism you have, breaking your nose like that on my forehead. You must have known that if there's one thing worse than an unconscious partner, it's a bloody one.' He tickled Colin coyly under the chin. 'You've done it before, haven't you?'

Colin stood, then fell over, then crawled on his hands and knees to his trousers. He was too angry to notice the target he offered and too upset to care. He pulled the vertebrae from the pocket, threw them onto the ground and started to pummel them again and again with a nearby rock. He shouted over and over again, 'Let's smash the bloody things and then please let me go home! I just want to go home.'

Nels took Colin tenderly by the arm and led him, still sobbing, back to their little camp.

He said 'Look, you cannot damage them. The only person who can is Mike Thom, the celestial grinder, grinder to the stars. I told you. Look,' he patted Colin comfortingly on the knee, 'we'll go to the town to try and make contact. I promise I won't touch you. You're obviously not much fun.'

Colin the Librarian, feeling cold comfort, got dressed rather shyly and started off with Nels towards the town which was now just a few hundred metres away (Colin realised that while they had stopped, the town must have been continuing to come over the horizon towards them). He stayed always three metres behind the knob-jockey. Why hadn't the Chronicles told of this champion's penchant for men? He suddenly chilled: only two weeks ago Susan the Social Worker had given FOCS a talk on this very subject: that at least three of the Chronicles' heroes were queer, Nels among them. How did she know so much? First she had known Krap's house was a mess, now it seemed she knew the sexual bent of a hero of the chronicle. He thrilled at the thought that Susan could be a visitor. She could come to him, could take him home. She could cuddle him, make everything all right and beautiful.

'Having second thoughts, honey?' asked Nels, spotting Colin's erection through his trousers and his awkward gait.

'No, no . . .' mumbled Colin, 'just a thought . . .'

'Hmmm, so I see,' mind-read Nels, 'though not a very pretty one,' he added cattily.

Colin was angry and Nels was rampant. They mutually accepted each other's state of mind as long as they kept their distance from each other.

# CHAPTER EIGHT

'What d'you want to know?'
Barman, Celestial Taverna, Cosmos Way

As they walked down the main street of the town, it suddenly struck Colin that this place, also, was deserted. He had spent – how many days was it now? – on this planet and was yet to come across any form of normal life. The resurgence of the Tharg quest for the vertebrae had really taken its toll on Threa, it seemed. He wondered for the umpteenth time how the FOCS fraternity would react to all this; then his mood slumped dramatically as he realised that it was odds-on that he would never see them again anyway, so who cared?

As they passed the unbroken rows of green brick, thatched roof, terraced houses that, but for the colour, could have introduced 'Coronation Street' (thought Colin), Nels came over and placed his hand gently on Colin's shoulder. Colin shuddered and tried to pull away, but the grip became vice-like.

'No, brave Librarian, do not shrink, for I have no carnal thoughts,' said Nels softly; at least his voice conveyed softness, but strength obviously lay just below the surface.

'I have read your mind for some time,' continued Nels of the Paulon, 'and am saddened by your desperation. But have hope. There is one whom we seek that must surely help you to dispose of the vertebrae and even return you to your land, for 'tis not impossible!'

Colin was stunned, and more than a little embarrassed. He looked up at Nels and almost pleaded.

'Who?'

Nels turned and pointed to what looked more like a Western saloon than a house, about a hundred yards down on the left. It was the only building to break the monotonous symmetry of the rows of houses that simply stretched into the distance forever.

'That, kind Librarian, contains the . . . ahhh!'

As Colin shifted his gaze from saloon to Nels, he realized to his astonishment that his companion was falling to the ground, his head split in two.

Colin heard himself ask, despite the rising panic and terror, 'What's an ahhh?' and immediately thought how stupid he sounded.

This went a little way towards breaking the spell and he managed to turn his head to look back the way they had come. He glimpsed a green cloak ducking into a doorway; the door slammed shut. Now, in blind panic, Colin tried to go in several directions at once. Pulling himself up off the floor, Colin turned and ran as fast as he could away from the still bleeding corpse and towards the saloon.

Amazed at his mind's capacity for blind terror and rational thought at the same time, (left and right hemispheres? he wondered), Colin burst through the swing doors at the entrance to the saloon, and collapsed on the floor, exhausted and hardly able to catch his breath. Through the pain of his lungs expanding to twice their normal size, Colin raised his head to look around.

It came as no surprise to Colin to see a Western-style bar. Everywhere he looked was wood; bar, stools, tables, doors, even wood panelling on the walls. It had the same green tinge as outside, but poor light (from just two candles on the bar and no windows) led to the feeling of being in a cave. It was cold and Colin shivered. The atmosphere was distinctly unfriendly.

Colin saw just one person sat at the bar. Slumped over, in front of a half empty bottle of vaqua wata (the equivalent of Earth whiskey but blue), the figure had its back to him. The clothes were rather ordinary, Colin thought but then he realized that what he meant was that they were rather normal for Earth; totally wrong for Threa. The black baseball cap was old and rather grubby, even in this light. The black sweater and badly fitting slacks seemed to be in a similar state. The feet were not covered. They were bare, showing bruises, corns and callouses.

Colin could see the pus oozing from the sores on these feet and started to feel sick. The slow, methodical squelch of the drops of goo hitting the floor made his throat close, restricting his breathing. Consequently, he screeched rather than spoke.

'Help me, please, help me! Nels sent me . . . Nels of the . . . Paulon . . . my name is . . . Ruth.'

This last statement, though at first sight blatantly untrue, was a noise as opposed to a name and signified Colin's collapse. He threw up all over the stranger's feet from no more than a yard away. The stranger slowly raised his head, shook his feet gingerly and got slowly off his stool. He turned to face Colin.

'You dirty bastard,' he muttered. His left foot suddenly shot out towards Colin's head, missed by several inches and the stranger swung round, crashed into the bar and slid gently to the floor. His head came to rest next to Colin's.

'Oh my God, I'm very sorry, sir, I mean I didn't mean, oh no! What have I done? Spare me. Sorry . . . sorry . . . sorry . . .' whimpered Colin. The stranger's eyes opened and he looked at Colin from six inches away in a dazed manner.

'Oh, that's OK then, Ruth. Just don't do it again and we'll forget it just this once.'

'No, my name's not Ruth, it's Colin. I'm on a quest and I really want to get home and I don't know how and who are you . . .?' Colin's mouth carried on moving, but no sound emerged. He looked like some actor in a silent movie, or the star of an odour-eaters ad. As his fish impressions calmed down, the stranger spoke again. No doubt about it this time, he was definitely drunk.

'I,' he said importantly, 'am Spasmo.' He waited for a response. After a pregnant pause, Colin replied.

'Oh, er, I am sorry, but I have never heard of you.' He continued, very puzzled, 'You don't appear in any of the ancient Chronicles which I know in minute detail. I really don't know you!'

Spasmo rather impatiently, snapped, 'Of course you do. Do you not recall Spasmo, Keeper of the Goals? Lessdick, siding with the Fives? Spider, Keeper of the Records? Me, mate. All me!'

Colin's mouth fell open. Yes, now he recalled all these. They had all, at various moments in the Chronicles mysteriously appeared and equally mysteriously disappeared. Spasmo was a . . . was a . . . and Lessdick had . . . um . . . Spider . . . Colin knew the characters and yet could not remember their roles or functions, or even what they were supposed to look like. As if they were shadows, they were there one minute, gone the next, leaving only the imprint of having been.

'Yep, all of them me,' slurred Spasmo proudly. 'I am as old as the hills, as new as a baby, as cunning as a Tharg, as desperate as a dump!'

He paused. 'No, I'm not,' he corrected himself.

'I beg your pardon?' said Colin, rather startled.

'Sorry, just another character trying to come out,' sighed Spasmo. His face started to contort slightly, and then straightened again, flushed from what had obviously been quite an effort. 'They do say that behind every successful man there's a good few dozen others. It's just that mine are inside, not behind. Tricky sometimes, but there you go!'

Colin's mind suddenly flashed brilliantly clear.

'Are you Mike Thom as well, celestial grinder to the stars?' he breathed excitedly, everything slotting into place.

'Yes, I am,' said Spasmo, then added, 'No, I'm not, and 'Yes, I'm not' and then 'Oh, bollocks!' and his head fell back to the floor again, his face contorting wildly. After a few seconds, he looked up and said, 'Sorry, sorry, Ruth. No I'm not. Never have been. Impossible. Mike Thom, I mean, not sorry. Of course I'm sorry but not Mike Thom. Someone else completely. Sorry.'

Colin stopped holding his breath and the escaping air whooshed into a series of sobs. His mind, having reached a peak of clarity and understanding, albeit of a small piece of a huge jigsaw, plunged headlong into the depths of despair.

'But I know a man who might know who is.'

Colin stopped blubbing and watched as Spasmo got up off the floor. He quickly followed suit, and found he was a good two feet shorter than Spasmo, whose skinny limbs hung like string from his black clothes.

'What?' asked Colin. 'Who?'

'Him,' said Spasmo. 'I mean you, I mean him; no, me, or her or not.' The face rippled violently, flapped a few times, then came to rest.

'Sorry. Got any ants?'

'Funnily enough, no,' snapped Colin, surprised at his sarcasm but infuriated by Spasmo's changing the subject. 'What for?'

'To wake him up. No, to go to sleep la, la . . . one flew over there and up and away . . . argh . . . get a grip,' groaned Spasmo, his face fighting yet another battle against itself before it calmed down again. He took a large swig from the half-empty bottle on the bar.

'Only damned way to keep it under control,' he said in response to Colin's gasp at the sight of one quarter of a bottle of vaqua disappearing in one swallow. Spasmo threw the bottle into the corner and there was a smashing sound, followed by a low moan. A bloated figure, Colin had not noticed before, pulled itself slowly to its feet from the dark corner where it had been resting. Rubbing its head, the figure staggered forward into the dim light. Colin recognized the dog-collar first, and then the swollen, fat features.

'Wealthy Vicars!' he gasped in amazement. His mind ran quickly through the stories of Wealthy Vicars' fight against the Mallows of the outlying Marshes of Threa; how they, in the absence of a Tharg empire, had tried to gain ascendancy in the universe.

The fact that the Mallows had no arms or legs and resembled leeches coloured purple and blue did not make their victory likely. They weren't helped by their lack of interstellar travel ability, indeed their lack of being able to travel anywhere at all. It was sometimes asked whether they had any yearnings to conquer Threa at all, as they never actually moved from the marshes. However, Wealthy Vicars' fight to tame them, ultimately converting them to Sylvestianity and getting their promise to stay in the marshes, for ever, was greatly publicised. Generally, Wealthy Vicars himself did the publicising, it must be said, but then who could argue with a man of the cloth?

'Yes, but they did bloody argue, didn't they?' slurred Wealthy Vicars, having followed Colin's thoughts through his drunken stupor. 'What's a bloke to do? This is the only place I can hide from the torment, the laughing; the accusations.

'OK, the Mallows were never really a threat in the real sense of the word, but then the point is that they never will be now, will they? All thanks to me. And how many people have stuck by me in all this? Fuck all. That's how many, fuck bleeding all.'

With this last profanity, Vicars collapsed across a table next to Colin. Spasmo spoke.

'Poor sod! Works himself stupid for two thousand years for the good of the planet and what reward does he get? Free booze for the rest of his life in a magical bar in the middle of town that doesn't really exist.' He paused. 'Pretty good deal when you think about it, I suppose!'

'But what are you doing here?' asked Colin, remembering the attack on Nels, and suddenly feeling uncomfortably close to being attacked himself. 'Why are you here? What did Nels mean when he said you could help?'

Spasmo straddled a chair and gently stroked the comatose head of Wealthy Vicars.

'Give us a kiss and I'll tell you,' he said with a resigned shrug in response to Colin's next thought. 'Yes, we had a relationship, but Wealthy never really responded. I made all the running.'

He looked at Colin, sighed again, and started to explain.

'I can read in your thoughts that the only references to me you found in the Chronicles were short and undefined, no real start, no real finish, just an appearance. That is how it should be, for each time I was trying to escape from the agony of my relationship with Wealthy. No, no, it wasn't really homosexual but I thought we really cared for each other sufficiently to go into business together and make a lot of money; maybe even enough to buy a small planet together, who knows?

'Anyway, without my knowledge or consent or anything, Wealthy ups and offs and starts this bloody marsh Mallows thing. Of course, having been through the Tharg Empire and its rule, Threans were naturally wary as to which life form would next rule the planet. The stories that Wealthy spread were accepted, and he was, as you know, hailed as a hero.

'Well, he didn't want to know me any more. No more wild parties or nights on the vaqua. He was living the high-life and I was barely scraping a living by changing identity occasionally and carrying out an *almost* brave deed. People just didn't pay much for the Lessdick running from the bloated Throbulets of Eelginmir, or Spasmo of the Goals achieving a lifelong ambition against all the odds of playing for Kotestrent and winning the league. No, what they wanted was someone who had saved them from another race. Someone like Wealthy Vicars.'

Colin recalled the references in the Chronicles to the celebration parties, the fêtes, the drink consumed when Threa was freed from a (as it now transpired) non-existent threat.

'But what happened?' Colin was puzzled. He knew that at the end of part 3 of the Chronicles, Wealthy Vicars was still at his most popular and commanded a good portion of the planet. He himself had role-played the character once, and enjoyed the associated power immensely. There had been no mention of Spasmo since he had won the league in Chapter one, but then Colin had been unaware of Spasmo's association with Vicars.

'Well,' continued Spasmo sadly, 'the Thargs returned and people looked to Vicars for help. He being just a fat, bloated twat, fled in terror. By sheer chance he found me here and we've been drinking ever since. The booze never runs out, so we never have to go out and we never do.' He ended with a shrug that said more than words and slumped back across the table, exhausted at having been coherent for three minutes.

Colin suddenly remembered Nels' end and glanced over at the door. Spasmo stirred. 'Don't worry, they never find this place. Bit surprised you did, really. Something about the optics outside, I think. Or inside. Not sure.'

Colin relaxed slightly, no longer surprised by anything that happened in this world. He remembered why he was here.

To answer your next question,' said Spasmo 'yes, Wealthy Vicars does know Mike Thom, grinder to the stars. They were good buddies once; not sure of the situation now, of course. But I think he knows when he hangs out.'

Colin was confused. This was all new to him. In his adventures to date, he'd had the (small) comfort of knowing where he was in the chronicles. But now he was on uncharted ground. His mind went into over-drive and an idea swirled tantalizingly in front of him, just out of his grasp. Spasmo threw a bottle at it and hit it (Colin's head). Suddenly Colin realized what was happening.

This was part four of the Chronicles. He was living it. No, he was bloody starring in it. My God!

'Who?' asked Wealthy Vicars.

Colin ignored him and tried to concentrate on his idea. If this was part four, someone must be writing it or were they? People write history after the fact. Who was the author? Someone who knew him? What was his destiny and where was Mike Thom? Someone, somewhere must know?'

For the first time in quite a while he felt in his pocket and pulled out the vertebrae. The rattling of the bones made Spasmo and Wealthy Vicars look up, and exclaim together 'Sylvester!'

# CHAPTER NINE

'Where can a god get a curry round here at this
time of the morning?'
Overheard speech by Sylvester, creative God
omnipresent.

For the first time in what seemed like weeks, Colin
managed to sleep unhindered and not due to con-
cussion. He had explained the background of his
adventure to date with the vertebrae to Spasmo and
Wealthy Vicars – all the way from that fateful afternoon in the library when Krap the Conqueror, larger
than life super-hero, had entered his life and the reference section. He honestly could not guess how many
days he had been on Threa. Every time he had been
knocked out or fainted, he had come round in an
unrecognizable place away from his black-out spot. He
could have travelled inches or miles. He couldn't say.

In his sleep, he mostly dreamt of the adventures he'd
had, all out of sequence but nevertheless complete. He
dreamt of the poor Ms Jackster, run through by a barbarian broadsword in the middle of Clacton Library.
Of Susan the Social Worker, caressing him gently on
the forehead, whispering softly, 'Colin, Colin, you
hunk! Wake up and give me one, Colin! Wake up,
Colin, I need you!'

His eyes opened slowly, trying to hold the image of
Susan leaning over him, her fingers making love to his
hair. He lost the battle, his eyes opened and he saw

Susan standing over him. He gasped. Closing his eyes tightly again, he still saw Susan in his dream. Only this time she was naked. He opened his eyes.

Looking around, the whole of his body except for one particular thing went completely loose. There was Susan sitting at a table with Wealthy Vicars and Spasmo. The three of them were silent and apparently sober. They looked at him with some interest. Susan looked at him strangely. Was that love? Or lust? Or disdain? Hatred even? Colin was all aflutter. He smoothed his jumper and trousers and remembered more of his adventures, as his caked underwear plucked the hairs from his lower regions and the smells of various bodily discharges washed up and over him. He was in no fit state to meet the dream-boat of his life, but his heart said Yes . . . Yes . . . go on, say something.

'Er . . . hello.'

Susan grunted and the other two giggled. Colin shuffled towards the table and saw that Susan wore an outfit similar to, if not the same as, that which she had used to portray a slave girl at a recent role-play exercise. (Of course Colin had gotten the part of Plebius the Poof, not the slave-master that he had prayed for, he remembered bitterly. Never the bloody slave-master when there was a slave that he wanted to . . .)

The two black-clad ex-super-heroes sniggered. They were obviously reading his mind and finding it funny. Susan slapped each of them across the face and turned to Colin.

'Banish impure thoughts, Librarian. Yes, 'tis I, Susan the Social Worker.'

'I thought that was a public decency offence,' blurted Wealthy Vicars, continuing to read Colin's mind, and both he and Spasmo exploded with laughter. Susan stood up, and flicked the table over into their faces.

This had the required effect. Both of them immediately became quiet and attentive. They got up off the floor, wiping splinters from their faces and went to sit at another table. Susan turned to Colin.

'You, Librarian, may continue to call me Susan. It is convenient. No more than that,' she added, seeing the fond look cross his face and feeling the glow in his brain.

Colin suddenly remembered what she had been saying whilst stroking his brow and hair. He couldn't really place whether 'Wake up and give me one' had been in his dream or in reality.

'In your dreams, sonny,' growled Susan.

Seeing her standing there, hands on hips, legs akimbo, that hard look on her face, he agreed and placed it in his dream towards the back of his mind. Maybe one day he would be able to confront her with his feelings . . .

'What are you doing here?' he asked her. 'How did you find me?' Her stance relaxed. 'I found you years ago on Earth, and have monitored your movements. For it was said that one of inconsequential size based in Clacton Library would unravel the answer to the mystery that is the Thargs and that is woven into the fabric of this very world.'

Colin felt quite proud of being mentioned in some fable or other.

Susan continued: 'I have bided my time and now feel it prudent to catch up with you. Pity about Krap, though.' She went misty eyed and looked distinctively moist at the thought of the Conqueror.

'So that's why you kept correcting some of our ideas and concepts at FOCS! Because you were actually *from* Threa,' said Colin excitedly.

'That's how you described Krap's waterhouse so accurately, and the furs in the corner and . . . ' Colin trailed off in mid-flow. Susan had gone glassy eyed again, and Colin thought he saw her knees tremble slightly. She obviously has a thing for Krap, he thought. Or rather *had* a thing. Colin felt intensely jealous. Why, if the Conqueror were here now he'd take him out and jolly well thrash him.

Susan sneered, reading his mind, and he snapped back to reality.

'We must move fast, Librarian, for 'tis only a matter of a few hours before the enemy find the entrance to the Celestial Bar of Eternal Condemnation. Then we shall be doomed. Now, have you the vertebrae?' She pushed her hand out and her 'slave' bangles rattled.

Colin dived into his pocket (or rather his hand did) and extracted the bones. But he had other ideas. Grasping them tightly he said, 'You obviously went from Threa to Earth and back. Send me back to Earth and I'll give you the bones.' He felt quite scared at his sudden show of strength.

'And what if I don't?' challenged Susan.

'Then I'll . . . I'll . . . I'll swallow them and stay here and be caught by the enemy and then I'll give them the . . . the vertebrae,' he said defiantly, quite impressed at the threat he had made up on spec.

'OK, hand them over and I'll send you back to Earth,' said Susan resignedly.

He passed the bones to Susan, who said with contempt, 'Prat! I can't send you back. I had a Return Sub-Spacial Cross Over, allocated by celestial blessing and only valid after six o'clock on days of the week beginning with the letter X in the fallopian alphabet. You are pathetic!'

Colin, soaring high with the notion of returning to Earth, came crashing back down to Threa. The only visible signs, it must be said, were the slump of his shoulders and tears running down his face. Was he more upset at Susan's attitude towards him or with being stuck on Threa for the rest of his life? Who cared? Maybe she'd learn to love him in time, he thought, grasping at very thin straws.

'Oh, stop crying,' scolded Susan. 'All is not lost.'

'Y-you mean there's a way to return, or that you could somehow come to love me?' sobbed Colin.

'There may, just may, be a way to return.' As if explaining to a child, Susan continued. 'You are in the fourth part of the *Chronicles of Threa, Ancient and Modern*. You are acting out the history of the planet.'

'So?'

'So someone must write and recite it.'

'So?'

'So,' said Susan impatiently, 'write the bloody thing. Get down to the task of recording each event that has happened from the end of part three to the present.'

'And?'

She punched him hard in the face.

'And you little bastard,' she screamed, 'write yourself back to bloody Earth at the end of the book. Be faithful in every detail, as the Chronicles can *never* lie, and you may just return. Sylvester! You are stupid.'

Colin rubbed his jaw and it clicked back into place with surprisingly little pain. His stomach was twisted by her rejection of his masculinity, but his heart was singing loud and clear.

'Home? I can go home? Oh, I love you Susan, I love you.'

'Yes, I know. But first we have to discuss the disposal of the vertebrae, for the Thargs will never leave you in peace until such a time as their hopes are destroyed.'

Suddenly Wealthy Vicars jumped up and shouted;

'I'll help you write it! I'll devote my life to you and your work. Oh, this is it. This is the biggy.'

Spasmo looked up at him and shook his head. He had a wry grin on his face.

'Never change, will you! Maybe that's why I love you!'

Wealthy Vicars stopped jumping around and said slowly, 'You mean that that night after the party when they found me with my underwear at half mast and you naked but for a loin cloth and Mike Thom being sick by the front door . . .' he tailed off. Spasmo nodded his head.

'Yes, it wasn't the drink that made him sick, it was the acts he had witnessed. Oh, I never meant for anyone to see, and I denied it all after and you were too drunk to remember, but . . .'

Wealthy Vicars was furious. 'I've told you before – bugger off and leave me alone. I'm bloody sick of you fawning around me in various disguises. Different characters, different faces, but always the same annoying git. Always trying to get your end away.' Now he was screaming. 'Now go away and die.'

Colin never thought that anyone could look as hurt as Spasmo did then. The man in black slowly got up, put his face in his hands and moved about a bit. Dropping his hands, they saw his face had changed. He had a huge nose, a small moustache and what sounded like a broad Yorkshire accent. He looked very, very sad.

'OK, OK, who are we now?' asked Wealthy Vicars, nodding.

'Guy Bloody Fawkenham,' shouted Spasmo sadly as he stretched out a finger and touched the candle on the wall.

As Colin started to say, 'Don't you mean Guy Fawkes?', the finger started to fizz and Spasmo shot up through the ceiling in a flash of light. Nothing could be seen of him. Colin was stunned.

'Good riddance,' said Wealthy Vicars, 'though I've no doubt the throbulet's gusset will be back.'

'Susan said . . .' started Colin and then fell into silence as Susan withered him with a stare.

'We'll manage better now,' she said.

Colin said, in disgust, 'How could you be so heartless? And you a Social Worker.'

'I'm not a social worker, I'm a super-heroine!' said Susan petulantly.

They were all startled by a confusing flurry of thought entering their minds. It's here somewhere, said one mind.

Probably some Celestial bar of Eternal Condemnation or something, came another thought.

Yeah, or a public bog.

There was laughter. 'Quick,' hissed Susan, 'Thargs! They are close. We must away.' She grabbed Colin's hand and dragged him through the wall, that appeared, conveniently and unsurprisingly to have grown a door. Wealthy Vicars bounced along behind, looking very scared.

As they emerged into the field, Colin looked back and saw nothing but more fields (par for the course on Threa, he thought, nothing strange there).

# CHAPTER TEN

'Haven't a clue, mate; try the environs of Jupiter, I
hear there's a load of food houses just opened
there. Open quite late too, I believe.'
Barman tittle-tattle with customer, Celestial
Taverna.

'**B**astards,' thought Yoof at the window, looking out
at the Keystone Cop activity below. He knew what
was going on all right. All the gods were getting
ready to leave the mountain and sally forth once more
into the world of mortal things. They sensed the weak-
ening of the Yoof twins, as did Yoof himself. Less and
less information came to him daily through the roots
and leaves of his domesticated dahlias as his plants
and trees and shrubs and those little pink flowers
that spring up absolutely anywhere were destroyed by
other life forms or by the elements. The mental screams
of dying vegetation kept him awake at nights. With his
brother still ailing he could not hope to repair the damage being done. It was a job for two fit, healthy gods,
not a cripple and a nursemaid, he thought bitterly.

Immediately scrubbing the thought from his mind,
he turned and looked fondly at his brother lying in the
bed, sleeping fitfully. Untilatelyoof stirred, and Yoof at
once put down the tray he held full of succulent fruit.
He soothed his brother's forehead and gently told him,
'I've brought up some breakfast.'

Yoof thumped his fist against the wall in frustration.
He just managed to catch it as it fell down. He yelled at

no one in particular: 'If you're going to build a bloody god a home then build it bloody stronger. I mean, it's not as if it's bloody difficult or anything. Just make the bricks a bit stronger and the cement and the bloody concrete. Sylvester! What d'you want, that I should write a bloody book about it?'

He stumbled as an incredible idea temporarily blinded him. Of course – books. The Book!

He threw his brother down the stairs and leapfrogged over him, narrowly beating the body to the bottom. Untilatelyoof registered nothing as he lay in a heap. 'Sorry, beloved brother,' floated back over his crumpled form.

Yoof had finally thought of how to contact this super-hero, this Librarian who was apparently the key to the survival of the planet world and therefore surely the *whole* world. He, Yoof, could not leave the mountain but he could create the messenger who *could* leave that sacred place of repose for the gods of creation. The messenger could be briefed, personally, by him to go forth, find Colin, bring him back and instruct him in the ways of ecology so that balance could be restored.

The first time, Yoof had not succeeded in communicating with the four horsemen of the puckered lips. But this would surely work. He had, on occasion, glimpsed the inner works of this Librarian's mind when Colin was in certain parts of the land and the atmospherics were OK. Yoof didn't begin to comprehend the hills that sung but he had recognized the Book.

It was exactly the same as the one that had come into his possession a long, long time ago. It was said that, having created the world, Sylvester himself had taken a rest and read this very Book, purloined from some distant galaxy, maybe, and written by some lost civilization. It was left on the ground when Sylvester departed, and legend had it that some of the first animal life actually worshipped it as his creation. It was handed on from generation to generation but had finally been taken to the gods who had demanded it, not wanting any false Gods or idols, nor idle Gods with falsies, to be worshipped because *they* were the number ones and they had created everything even though nobody remembered their names or where they were or even that they still existed.

The Book was full of strange runes and pictures that the gods didn't understand owing to the fact that they were illiterate. But there was now a definite link with Colin. Yoof saw that clearly. He should use it to create a messenger who would be acceptable to and understood by this Colin the Librarian.

Pushing into the communal latrine where the Book was kept for some obscure reason (nobody knew why, it just seemed a good loo read), Yoof found the god Thickun, trousers down, sitting on the toilet browsing through the Book.

'Pray, oh mighty one, give us the Book as I sorely do have need of it, yea,' cried Yoof and he snatched the Book from a startled Thickun.

'Oi! What's your game? I had it first. I haven't finished with it yet,' protested the Thickun. 'Give it back, I tell thee.' Injured innocence gave way to anger as it became clear that Yoof was not listening. He was too busy thumbing through the Book as he went towards the door. 'Give it back! Foorsooth, I prithee, you git,' yelled the constipated god still with his trousers down.

Getting no response, Thickun created a blue glob of

obviously primaeval life of fundamentary construc-
tion, and hurled it at Yoof, who just caught the
movement out of the corner of his eye and ducked in
time to allow the glob to smear itself across the far
wall. Yoof ran from the room as a repulsive wave of
noxious gases exploded from Thickun's untrousered
posterior.

'Excuse me,' grumbled Thickun sourly as he settled
down to finish his ablutions without the Book. 'Bloody
Yoofs of today. There's no telling you, is there? All that
bloody fauning and floraing about. We'll show you!
Ha, You wait!' he yelled after him.

Yoof sat down on the comatose body of his brother.
Ah! There it was. He had found the photo of the three
people. He folded the Book open, almost breaking the
spine. That's it. Now, he just had to create these, and
they would be sure to locate Colin and bring him back
to him toot sweet.

By holding the Book hard he caught a mental
glimpse of a person sat in an cubby-hole, moist hands
gripped around . . . around the hard back edition of . . .
of the latest fantasy novel epic. The person looked
excited. His trousers throbbed and his forehead per-
spired. Then . . . there was an older person . . . a female
of the species, looking on.

'What does Colin see in those sword and sorcery
novels that could excite a young, thrusting man to . . .
oh, my gosh, to do that sort of thing,' was written
all over her face. She had failed to notice the multi-
coloured pictures of *National Geographic* lying
within the pages of the adventure hardback.

The Book – so it did come from the Librarian himself. Great Sylvesters! Yoof hurriedly took a handful of
soil from the plant pot in front of him and put it on the

floor. He split it into three equal piles and placed the Book over them, photo down.

Raising his arms he threw back his head and started to mumble, fingers waving. There was a flash, a roll of thunder, a crackle of lightning and the Book burst into flames. Nothing out of the ordinary there – the usual creation business.

Yoof was stamping out the fire on his brother's clothes when the three green pods left behind in the ashes of the Book split open like bananas. There stood three people, exactly the same as he had seen in the book. Three small yet perfectly formed pygmies, looking round in incredulity.

'Not bad for a God of Flora and Fauna,' he crooned as he surveyed his handiwork. 'Now all I have to do is teach them to talk and they can deliver my message.' He was rubbing his hands together as he ushered them into the front room away from the choking smoke still coming from the stair carpet. he had a nagging feeling that maybe the picture had not been full size and he should have created them bigger. And that staple in the head of the middle one would have to go.

Four months later they were ready. They had names, and a message to deliver to one Colin, the Librarian:

'Greetings, Oh Mighty Mortal, from the god Yoof, creator of all things green and other colours and beautiful bounteous. Thee art summoned, oh Librarian, to the god's abode. Be not shy. Thou are to be taught how to restore ecological balance to this once proud and mighty planet. Thine time ist come, oh mighty one. Thou art summoned.'

They rehearsed this morning and afternoon until the

pygmies were word perfect . . . most of the time. Not bad for a bit of ad-lib, thought Yoof as he listened with increasing pleasure to the godly pronouncement that would surely rush his hero to him.

# CHAPTER ELEVEN

'ZZZZZZZZZZZZZZZZZZZZZZZZZZZZZZZZZZZ
ZZZZZZZZZZZZZZZ'

Quote from Sylvester, the God, early on Friday
morning.

'Tell me,' Colin gasped to Susan as she dragged him
along at great speed. 'Do we always emerge into
the same field, or into different ones?'

He was half cracking a joke, but Susan answered
seriously.

'There are several exit points on the planet; all into
fields. This one is close to the Birches of Cumber and
Marvel, home of Mike the Thom.'

As the three companions slowed to a walk, Colin
pointed to a huge building in the distance.

'Is that it?' Colin gasped.

'Yes,' said Susan, 'but he won't be there. The Thargs
would have searched The Birches first to try to capture
him and stop him grinding the vertebrae, should they
ever get to him. All we're likely to find are clues to his
whereabouts. Come on, we'll have to break in.'

A figure approached them as they walked towards
the hall, a vast Tudor thing. (The hall, not the figure.)

At least eight full-length windows, painted grey,
looked out from each of three floors. The walls were
blue, and the wooden beams that criss-crossed them
were red. Some of the angles created by the beams
were virtually impossible but for all that it looked

sturdy enough. Some beams even crossed some of the windows, giving a barricaded and nailed-up look to the property.

The man, who stopped a few yards away from them and some fifty yards or so from the house, was dressed from top to bottom in brown. Brown balaclava, brown sports coat, brown sweater, brown cords and brown brogues. The sports coat even had brown leather patches on the elbows, noted Colin with approval.

'Who are you?' shouted Susan rather too loudly.

'Batten, keeper of the Hatches, and gardener to my lord master, Thom.' He spoke in a strange, rural accent.

'I thought you were a Tharg,' sniggered Wealthy Vicars and immediately fell sideways as he was punched in the temple by Susan.

Suddenly this was all too much for Colin, who lurched forward and started to wave his arms in manic fashion. 'Just hold everything,' he said, 'that's enough.'

He had just spent the last half hour or so digesting Susan's suggestion that, in order to get home, he write the saga of the fourth part of the Chronicles. It would have to incorporate all this new plot and she would rip his balls off if he got any of it wrong. Anyway, it was disillusioning to find that these were heroes or super-heroes or heroines were in it just for the fame and fortune that it brought them. Still he had to get home.

A bath or shower at this stage would probably have the same effect on him that Susan used to, before he discovered her true persona and started to wish that her husband had smacked some humility into her during her stay on Earth. But now, he was sure they were taking him for a ride.

'How many characters are we going to meet?' he

shouted at Susan. 'How many am I going to have to remember? I've got to write this stuff up and get it all right before I can get home, and all you seem to be doing is going off to meet new people that don't really count, but just add to the confusion.'

'But this is Mickey Thom's house; you need him to grind the vertebrae before you can start writing the book. What's the problem?' asked Wealthy Vicars.

'He's not bloody here, is he?' shouted Colin, exasperated. 'She said he wouldn't be here and he isn't! So why are we bloody here? Meeting Batten, the bloody Hatches, just to piss me off, that's why.'

Susan brought her foot down hard on Colin's toes. He hopped about in anger and pain while she scolded.

'Pull yourself together, wimp. We're here to find out where Mickey Thom is. Where he's got to.' She turned to Batten.

'Where is he? Where's the Grinder, your master? We have a package for him.'

Colin, with some glimmering of understanding what Susan was up to and a thumping pain in his foot, calmed down. Batten thought a moment, as if weighing them up, then spoke slowly in what to Colin sounded like his father's version of a Yorkshire accent.

'His mastership's told me to say nowt, lest he be incriminated against his previous employers and friends the Thargs, and in particular against the three that threatened to kill him and what's that package, anyway?' He paused for breath.

Susan fumbled for a second in her (ample, thought Colin, old feelings revived) cleavage and, with Wealthy Vicars fidgeting uncomfortably, drew out a sparkling chain of vertebrae. Batten's mouth dropped open, and he fell to his knees, arms in the air.

'Oh Sylvester! Oh no, oh no, oh gosh!'

'That's why we need him. Where is he?' demanded Susan.

''D-d-down at the Old Priory of the Good Fellowship, where the bull would face the swan with a bell at its station, and the crown of roses is heaped on the polar bear's spring bank and the . . . '

'OK, OK, I know where it is. Have you been drinking?' Susan cut him off mid-flow.

A window opened in the first floor of the mansion and an unseen girl cried, 'Batty! Batty! Come here please, and bring me your pecker, now. I'm nice and cosy and waiting.'

Batten of the Hatches, still on his knees, shouted 'Coming, Betty, my dear, willy and all.' He shuffled off on his knees towards the huge front door.

Suddenly their minds were invaded by a wave of aggression. They instinctively turned, and saw six or seven green clad Berserkers, Tharg stormtroopers, rushing at them. Wealthy Vicars screamed, Colin did himself yet another mischief, and it was left to Susan to lead the group with some degree of sanity. Eerily, the only sound was the thumping of the Berserkers' feet and the plopping of collapsing heads as spines were drawn, ready for action.

'They must have followed us. Quick, run in opposite directions. Split up and try to make it to the house. Quick!'

Everything about the directions taken by Colin and Wealthy Vicars were so opposite that they crashed together where Susan had stood just a few seconds earlier. Colin bounced off the tubby form and just had time to register relief before accompanying Wealthy Vicars on the slide to oblivion, by now a welcome friend.

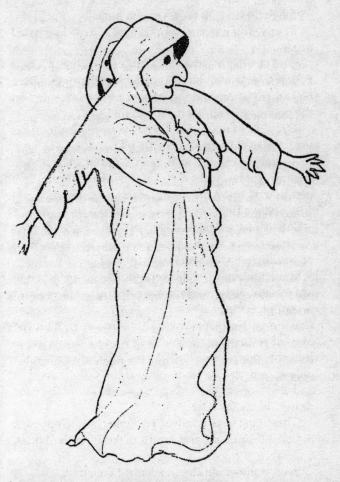

## THARG BERSERKER
*Note that the back of the two heads usually went around in quite a jovial, even theatrical frame of mind while the other did all the serious stuff like mind control and pulling the other's spine out to throw at enemies.*

When Colin came back to consciousness his brain felt like a soft sponge three times as big as the head that contained it. He found he was in a bare stone room of some kind. It had no furniture and was built of green stone. There was a door (closed) but Colin didn't know how long it would stay that way.

He sat back down on the floor and went over events again. He must have escaped from the Berserkers, but how? A horrifying thought struck him; maybe he had been captured. Maybe the others were dead. Wealthy Vicars and . . . and . . . and . . .

'Susan!' he cried, ' My Susan! Dead . . . Oh God . . . Susan. Wait, I shall join you. I forgive you for your attitude. You were under pressure. Oh, Susan, we are star-spangled lovers. Are we fated to be parted forever?'

He repeated her name over and over as he searched for something in the cell to use in his suicide bid. he could find nothing, and banged his fists on the door in frustration.

The door suddenly opened inwards. Colin was blasted across the room. His head smashed against the wall and once again he fell into the pitch black of nothingness.

# CHAPTER TWELVE

'Look, you can't sleep here, mate, it's private
property and I'll probably get closed down for
harbouring vagrants. Oh, what's the use? See you
in the morning.'
Desperately tired barman, Celestial Taverna,
Cosmos Way.

As he came to he heard Susan's soft voice say, 'Colin, Colin the Librarian, I want you . . . ' Oh, no, not again, he thought, '. . . to get up and stop farting about! How was I to know that you were behind the door? There's plenty of room in here without having to choose the door to hide behind.' Her voice, however, did reveal a hint of emotion, and it wasn't lost on Colin. He went all gooey.

He got up to see Susan and Wealthy Vicars staring at him, together with a puny little specimen some inches shorter than Colin.

'Who're you?' asked Colin.

'Mickey Thom,' answered the specimen in a squeak.

'But,' said Colin looking at Susan, 'how did we get away from the Thargs?'

'She did a spell!' chanted Wealthy Vicars. Susan, was looking very smug.

'Chapter four, page 793, volume 2 of the Chronicles, Colin,' she recited.

The sponge in his head instantly turned back to a brain and he remembered. 'And yea, verily, they that do right shall have one chance only at a spell. And that spell may be such that it shall, with the concentration of cosmic forces that do swirl and move clouds of noxious gases that await a happening in the eons of time rid the immediate area surrounding the blessed individual of they whom are without trust. Yea, verily are they completely without any form of doubt whatsoever of the immediate place and time continuum and they are forever hereinafter referred to as the licencee to be empowered to keep the grass free of all undesirable creations.'

Colin had never really understood that bit, and had never found anyone that did.

'Blimey! You understand that and used it?' said Colin in even greater admiration.

'No,' admitted Susan, 'I just held out the vertebrae to give them to the Thargs, who looked at them and . . .'

'And all their spines shot out!' yelled Wealthy Vicars.

'And all their spines shot out,' confirmed Susan.

'And they all folded up!' continued Wealthy Vicars.

'And they all . . . just shut up, Vicars – you weren't even there! Yes, they all folded up and turned into a writhing mass of steaming jelly. And then, when Wealthy Vicars came round, we carried you here. You should do something about that smell, you know.'

'But . . . that's magic!' exclaimed Colin, mightily impressed.

'Yes,' squeaked Mickey Thom, 'but it will only work twice. Once for each set of vertebrae. Vincent had told Susan about it a long time ago, and quite frankly I'm surprised that she remembered.'

Colin couldn't help thinking that that was a heck of a squeak.

'Of course!' he suddenly remembered, 'I saw you at the palace at Kotestrent! You were one of Vincent's

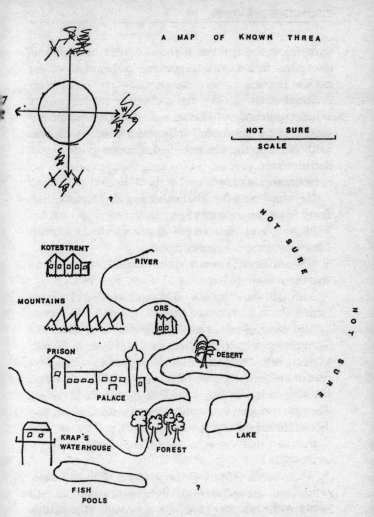

NOT SURE

SCALE

NOT SURE

NOT SURE

KOTESTRENT

RIVER

MOUNTAINS

ORS

PRISON

DESERT

PALACE

LAKE

KRAP'S
WATERHOUSE

FOREST

FISH
POOLS

*This is a map of THREA, drawn by Colin entirely from memory. He has tried to show the sites of all his adventures, but unconsciousness prohibits accurately depicting the bits in between, or indeed the scale.*
*The bits not drawn may or may not exist.*

girls! Now I remember, there was something strange about that collection, but I couldn't quite put my finger on it at the time.'

Susan blushed. 'Yes, I did disguise myself as one when I returned from Earth, in an effort to keep an eye on the vertebrae. Then I followed you when you left with Nels of the Paulon.' She stopped with a self-satisfied grin.

Colin was stunned, and walked around in a small circle wondering how he was going to write this up. How many other subterfuges didn't he know about? How long had he been there? He suddenly remembered the reason for being here.

'The vertebrae! Give him the vertebrae! He can grind them and I can go home!'

'Calm down, calm down,' squeaked Mickey Thom, 'it's all done. I have used the celestial pestle and mortar to grind all six into dust. Never more shall the Tharg Empire rule!' His voice grew louder to a trimphone pitch. 'Never more shall vile Andrew the Spineless be Andrew the Spineful. See how the suns shine. See the pretty birds – hear their song. They rejoice! They rejoice! See the beautiful waff waff . . .' Mickey Thom trailed off into a series of coughs. The emotion was obviously too much for him. He left the room.

'Where's he going?' asked Colin.

'Back to Mickey Thom's palace,' replied Susan. 'There is no danger now. All Berserkers will have died along with their last chance of survival in the future. They will all have pulled their spines out at the agony piercing their brains following the grinding of Andrew the Spineless's vertebrae. I must away to a life in better parts, to tell everyone of my success and to sell vertebrae dust at ninety spondus a packet. And I suppose that you and Wealthy Vicars had better start writing that book if you want to get home. Why not stay here and write? No one's using the place.'

Susan looked at Colin with definite fondness, and he was sure she was about to kiss him when their minds were suddenly, and silently shattered by the mental scream of a body in pain; terrible pain.

A huge crimson shape appeared around the door. It was Thong the Third. Two heads had already collapsed. The right hands fought to complete the suicide by pulling out the final spine. The left hands fought them off! He staggered forward and screamed aloud:

'You bastards! I could have had it all . . . I was so near to you . . . Do you realize what you've done?'

Suddenly the spine was plucked from the third neck. As the head collapsed, the spine was thrown, and as the body twitched in death, Susan was impaled. Blood was everywhere, green mingling with red as Susan collapsed.

Wealthy Vicars was the first to move as he ran up to Thong and kicked the prone sack of bubbling Tharg flesh.

'Take that, you bastard, and don't ever do that again,' he shouted.

The movement broke the spell, and Colin dropped to his knees and cradled Susan's head in his lap, gently stroking her brow, and taking the opportunity to stroke her now still breast. Her body lay like a hump-backed bridge, macabrelly speared by a Tharg back bone, which even now started to crumble. As she twitched, Colin for one fleeting second thought she was alive. Alas, she was not. Her eyes were glazed, blood ran from her mouth, and Colin cried. He cried for almost a year, such was his sadness.

He was, of course, doing other things as well during that year. He and Wealthy Vicars set to writing *The Chronicles of Threa; Ancient and Modern, Volume four*. Mickey Thom's palace was a vast catacomb of rooms, all of which looked alike. There were hundreds of passages and corridors, and Wealthy Vicars and Colin kept on getting lost which hindered the writing. On several occasions they lost each other for a week as one set out to ask the other a question. They had decided to write various bits each in separate rooms to avoid the other's smell and annoying little habits.

When the Tharg meat ran out, they ate Susan (Colin apologized first), and when she ran out they lived on berries, nuts, leaves, with the odd passer-by thrown in for flavour.

One day Colin was out taking the air in the garden when he heard a voice squeak at him.

'Are you . . . um . . . Colin the Librarian?' it asked.

Looking down in surprise, Colin gasped. Three pygmies stood in front of him, each about six inches high.

'You're pygmies, aren't you?' he exclaimed, a stupid grin on his face.

'Buggered if we know,' squeaked one before repeating his question.

'Yes, I'm Colin . . . er . . . Colin the Librarian . . . haven't I seen you somewhere before? I'm sure I have, you know.' Colin stood, chin on hand, looking hard at the three in front of him. He frowned heavily, trying to remember. Three pygmies: two men and one woman with . . . Colin blushed . . . with those sort of cone-shaped um breasts with er huge um thingies.

'Breasts,' he exclaimed suddenly as the startled pygmies jumped back. 'Oh, um sorry,' he said, blushing, 'I mean, I recognize you. I know you from the *National Geographic*. You were in that issue 2 IV part 4. About the same size too,' he mused. 'I wonder what happened to that copy? I remember putting it down on top of the thriller Section when Ms Jackster caught me in the storeroom . . . ' he went scarlet . . . 'I mean um I was just you know reading about your breasts . . . um about er you about him and you and your people and er . . .' he stumbled on, 'and er, I've never seen it since. Vanished off the face of the earth, as it were! Well, well! Fancy that!'

The pygmy in front gathered up his courage and took a step forward.

'Are you . . . ah . . . Colin the Whasitsname?'

'Yes. I've already told you, I'm Colin the Librarian.'

The second male pygmy chipped in, 'He'll do. The name rings a bell, actually.'

'Who are you three, then?' asked Colin.

The first pygmy pushed his chest out proudly.

'I,' he screeched, 'am Anthony, son of William. He,' and he pointed to the other male, 'is William, son of Anthony. And er, I think she's er ah yes, William's aunt Toni.' The others nodded sagely.

William's aunt Toni looked up at the sky, and saw the three red suns at various stages of setting over their various horizons. She tutted.

'Is that the time already?' she trilled. 'Time we weren't here, I'd say.'

The men nodded agreement and unfolded green, sleeping-bag type things from their back-packs. Laying them on the ground they got into them.

'What on Earth are you doing?' Colin demanded.

'Bedding down, it's called,' responded Anthony, son of William. He further zipped his pod shut. 'We do it every day; go to sleep just before dark, and wake up just after dark's gone. All plant life does it, you know. Anyway, I *think* it gets dark,' he stifled a yawn, 'I've never actually seen it get dark, because I'm always in here. But I'm told it does. I think. See you later.' The pod shut.

Colin didn't move for a few seconds. He just stared at the three green pods, each about seven inches long laying on the ground before him. What did he mean, all plant life? Pygmies aren't plants.

The pods didn't move and didn't look like they were going to, so Colin sat on the ground next to them, wondering what to do. It is quite late, he thought, as he yawned and lay down. In no time at all he was asleep.

Colin woke up to an awful smell of rotten manure, that reminded him of uncle's roses. He felt disoriented and suddenly thought he was in the hands of the Thargs again. It was the smell of fear, as he readily recognized from some of his earlier adventures. He opened his eyes warily, and then sat up in amazement.

The three pygmies stood there, squatting in front of him. They were defecating a manure-like substance. Every so often they would stop and eat a handful.

'What in heaven's name are you doing?' gasped Colin, trying not to breathe the smell in through his nose.

Anthony, son of William . . . or was it William son of Anthony? . . . or anyway one of them answered him.

'The slow hand crap ceremony, oh mighty . . . um thingy the whatsit.' The other one chipped in, 'What comes from the soil returns to the soil and enriches our surroundings. We are honouring thee, oh mighty one!'

Colin was amazed and disgusted at the same time. He had never read anything in his magazines about pygmies doing this sort of stuff. He thought they ate things like witchitty grubs and snakes. Well, fair's fair, he thought, I don't exactly read the articles very thoroughly, it's more a case of looking at the . . . h'mm, well. Maybe this is normal for them. No, it couldn't be.

'That looks revolting!' he said with distaste and little regard for the rituals of a primitive people. The pygmies wiped their hands on the ground, having apparently completed the ceremony.

'Bye then,' said William, or Anthony, or anyway, not aunt Toni. He extended his hand towards Colin who automatically grasped and shook it before realizing what he had done.

'Where are you going?' asked Colin as the three moved off.

'Something to do,' answered the woman as they paused. She turned to the men. 'Good point, actually, where are we going?'

'Dunno,' said one of them, who then turned to Colin. 'Are you Colin the thingy?'

'We've been through all this,' said Colin exasperatedly. 'I'm Colin the Librarian, christened by Krap the mighty Conqueror.'

'Oh yes,' squeaked the other one, 'that's it, it's you, isn't it. That's right, got it now. Fine.'

There was a pregnant silence before Colin asked 'Were you looking for me?' He was still puzzled.

'Why, who are you?' queried aunt Toni.

Colin yelled, 'I've told you a hundred times, I'm Colin . . .'

'H'mm, sounds familiar, now that you say it,' mused one of the pygmies in a high-pitched whine. He clicked his fingers and they fell off. Colin was thunderstruck to see them immediately blossom and bloom into beautiful flowers. He was even more gobsmacked to see new fingers start rapidly to grow on the man's hand. His mouth fell open.

'Yes, that's it,' said the pygmy carefully, 'we've found you. It is, isn't it?'

'What?'

'You.'

'Me?'

'Yes, you!'

'Um, yes, it is, I suppose.'

'Good,' said the little man, nodding his head knowingly. 'Good!'

There was another long break punctuated only by the nodding head. The pygmy interrupted it.

'Fine! Bye then!'

As they moved away, Colin called them back.

'Why were you looking for me?'

'Ah, yes,' said one in response, 'yes, good point.'

'Message!' trilled aunt Toni. 'A message!'

'Yes,' chimed the others. 'We've got a message for you.'

Colin shivered in anticipation. He wasn't sure whether fear or excitement was the cause.

'A message for me?'

'Yes! For you.'

'Who from?'

The pygmies looked at each other, silent.

'You know,' said one, 'from Yoof.'

'Who's Yoof?'

'You know, Yoof . . . Yoof's Yoof,' jeered the pygmies.

'No, I don't know Yoof. I don't know anyone by that name.'

'OK, OK, see you then.'

Colin was getting very annoyed now. He stamped

his foot and the pygmies fell over. 'So what's the flipping message then?' he demanded.

'Oh yes, the message,' said the pygmy, brushing some imaginary specks of manure from his buttocks. 'Um . . .' he turned to the others. 'Any of you like to give the message?' They both shook their heads.

'No', trilled aunt Toni, 'you go right ahead. No problem. All yours. Thanks anyway.'

'Ah!' said the speaker. He turned back to face Colin. 'Um . . . the message is . . . it is . . . very long and er starts with . . . um . . . whatsit. You know, that thing.' He looked embarassed.

'What thing?' asked Colin menacingly, the words crawling out from gritted teeth.

'Er . . . Greetings! Yes, that's it, greetings. Then it goes . . . um tee dum, tee dum, the something dee dah thingy.'

'There's an ecology in it,' added aunt Toni helpfully, but rather vaguely.

'Oh yeah, greetings ecologically . . . dee dum tanh tanh and the rest of it. I think that's it.'

'Hang on,' said Colin disbelievingly. 'You've got a message for me and you can't remember it? Well?'

The message relayer squeaked indignantly back. 'We only bloody learned to talk a few weeks ago. You expect us to be perfect in everything? We've given you the gist of the message. Ecological greetings and wosname. That's it, I think.'

Colin advanced menacingly.

'Why, you little . . . *what's the message . . . pip squeak*?'

'Stand back,' squeaked the pygmy in terror. 'I've got a blow pipe and I'm not afraid to use it!' He fumbled a blow-pipe from his back-pack and held it out towards the advancing Colin. The others did the same, their faces showing a mixture of fear and determination. They closed into a tighter defensive formation.

'I said' continued Colin slowly, 'give me the message. Think hard, you idiots.'

'We're bloody good shots, you know,' warned the pygmy as they all put darts in their blow-pipes, and raised them to their lips. Colin called their bluff and came nearer. He squeezed his eyes shut as he saw three sets of cheeks puff and three darts, probably poison-tipped, he thought, were ejected.

The pinpricks of pain signalling instant death never came. Colin warily opened one eye in time to see a huge ostrich-like bird plummet from the sky. The three darts sticking out of its head gave it an obscenely comic look as it fell onto the pygmies with a dying squawk, and crushed them.

Little arms and legs twitched grotesquely as the life force left them in a hurry. Colin felt so upset that he forgot completely about the ungiven message. He had actually started to grow quite fond of these little people, even if they were very frustrating at times.

This was soon tempered by satisfaction that he could now stock the larder with bird flesh and pygmy delicacies.

Colin worked on the early bits of the Chronicle. Along the way he recalled many sad occasions and the passing of what he realized, with hindsight, were good friends.

Wealthy Vicars wrote the latter bits that he had been involved in and supplied the fancy artwork.

Life was not exactly idyllic, but it was the best that Colin had enjoyed for some considerable time. He had little trouble in keeping the language similar to that used in the previous volumes. He did, after all, know them by heart.

He used alot of 'And yea, verily it came to pass that' and 'happen as maybe that it did occur that . . .' and even 'the mist descended and all was darkness until the resonance of the chorus did stir the mighty Librarian . . .' with a lot of poetic licence. Colin had time to reflect on the changes in his character. He was pained at the remembrance of what he had been in Clacton – an under-developed, weedy, socially backward little toe-rag, really. The change in diet to all things natural and Threan, had put some meat on him to the extent that he was now wiry as opposed to skinny. He was also a lot less ready to take lip from anybody. His character had been formed by his close proximity to death, he decid-ed. Either that or the fact that anyone who makes a mess in his trousers with such regularity and in such volumes, *had* to become indifferent to public opinion. He still cried a little whenever he thought of Susan, but the feeling was fading by the day and he decided that he would turn into a wild, raging sex machine on his return to Clacton. This would help him forget.

Wealthy Vicars also thrived in this time. From being a giggling fat prat, he became merely a giggling plump prat. Although he came over as very simple, Colin always felt a little uncomfortable in his presence – as if he was hiding something . . . something slightly evil . . . anyway . . .

Then came the day. Colin and Wealthy Vicars were holding their 'Weekly Status and Reference meeting'. Each meeting was minuted and the minutes filed in the makeshift filing racks erected by Colin during his unexpected 'handyman' phase. Each shelf, in fact, was the rib cage of the Tharg, of Susan and three of the passers-by he and Wealthy had to eat during the year.

The Chronicles were now bang up to date and required just one word to be complete.

'And yea verily then did Colin return . . .'

On the insertion of the word 'home' then, Colin would presumably flash back to Earth and continue his life. He desperately wanted to remember everything but accepted that his adventures might be erased from his mind as these things always seem to be in the films he'd seen on TV.

They thought about him taking a copy of the Chronicles with him so that he could re-read everything, but decided that copying them out (1394 pages to date) would take just about as long as inventing the photocopier.

They agreed that when Colin had gone, Wealthy Vicars would take a year's sabbatical and tour the planet to update the situation generally outside the confines of the Priory. He would then return and complete the Chronicles with a description of life post-Tharg threat. Colin also agreed that Wealthy Vicars could claim all copyright and marketing rights on volume 4.

'Don't you want me to send you some money?' asked Wealthy Vicars, that gleam in his eyes again, adding insincerity to the question.

'What the hell would I do with three bags of goat droppings, four porcupines and a chicken's leg?' demanded Colin, hands on hips, jaw thrust out and muscles flexed, though you wouldn't have noticed. The list he had recited was half of what Wealthy Vicars had reckoned he could guarantee in royalties in the first six months. Colin was sure he meant concubines but Wealthy was insistent that it was four porcupines.

'Those things with the sharp edges,' Colin had said. 'That's not a hell of a lot, is it?' to which Wealthy Vicars replied, glint in eye again, 'Well, maybe the odd sheckell, schmekkel, goat dung, who's checking?'

Well . . . Wealthy Vicars was ready to inscribe the word 'home' and Colin was ready to go. Suddenly his mind was flooded by doubt. Where would he land? Did he really no longer smell, or was it just that he had got used to it? He hadn't brushed his teeth in a year. Halitosis! Don't breathe on anyone. Money . . . If he landed in Scotland or something how did he get home?

Wealthy Vicars lent him ten Threan farts, one of which equalled one twentieth of a spondu, but this went no way to putting Colin's mind at rest. All his new-found composure was lost.

'Oh God, what now? What can I do? I can't stay here. Please do something,' Colin ranted.

Wealthy Vicars had turned back to the manuscript on the table constructed from layers of skin stretched over the arm bones and the legs made of leg bones. Wealthy turned round to face him.

'I'm sick of your ranting. I've just completed the sentence. Goodbye forever, wimp. Ha, ha, ha, ha!'

Colin screamed. Nothing happened.

'Shit!' muttered Wealthy Vicars under his breath as he went over to Colin. 'Um . . . only kidding, guv, um . . . great. You're still here. Super . . . have a nice trip? Very short I see, er . . . how is the old place? Oh Sylvester!'

That was it. Colin collapsed and cried and cried and cried.

'I knew it wouldn't work! Damn you, Susan! Damn you for the false hope. I'm bloody glad I ate you.

Damn, damn, damn you.'

He started to beat his head on the floor in frustration and desperation. He saw blood spatter onto the stone. He said hello to that long-lost friend oblivion.

He came to . . . He looked up hazily into Wealthy Vicar's eyes.

'I think I've got it, Librarian, I think I know what went wrong.'

Colin got groggily to his feet and it all came rushing back to him. 'What? What went wrong?' he mumbled.

'Something's not right!' said Wealthy Vicars hurriedly.

'I know that, idiot,' snapped Colin, 'I'm still here, aren't I?'

'No, no, I mean there must be some historical innacuracy in the Chronicle that we've written. Something small, OK, but nevertheless something that's not right. All we have to do is find it!'

'Oh, is that all?' scorned Colin. He continued sarcastically, 'Well we'd better get reading again, then hadn't we?' As Wealthy Vicars walked past Colin on his way to the manuscript, Colin caught him square on the jaw with the best (and the only) right hook he had ever thrown. As Wealthy Vicars slid down the wall, he mumbled, 'What was that for?'

'You know, you bastard,' muttered Colin, rubbing his knuckles.

The next few months went by very, very slowly, as the two untrusting companions went through the drafts page by page, word by word, to see if any mistakes had been made.

Rows erupted, each blaming the other and eventually leading to one or the other storming off for three or four weeks.

### SUSAN THE SOCIAL WORKER
*Colin used Susan's skull and lots of mud to reconstruct her features as a model for the study portrait in still life. (Hence the exposed vertebrae below the scarf.)*
*The potatoes remind Colin that she is still very much in his body and soul because he ate her.*

Various small errors were rectified. Krap, they found, was not always spelled with a capital K. Thargs was sometimes written 'Thrags'. Wealthy Vicars had to agree that he did not destroy the Tharg Berserkers single handed . . . little things like that which, though maybe in the end important, were not the corrections required.

By now it was late autumn and the trees were starting to fall (Colin was not entirely sure that the whole tree should fall as opposed to simply the leaves as on Earth, but Wealthy Vicars assured him it was perfectly normal on this part of Threa). The rooms were turning cold. One day the pair were polishing off the last of the Throbulet caught in their home-made 'rib-cage' trap when Colin choked. When Wealthy Vicars had finished slapping his back, Colin grunted,

'Page numbers!'

'What?' asked Wealthy Vicars, only slightly interested.

'Page numbers. We haven't put any page numbers on it. That must be it. We know how many pages there are, but we haven't numbered them. Let's do it.'

Wealthy wasn't convinced that this was the solution, but they divided the pages into two and Colin started numbering up, and Wealthy started numbering down.

When Colin ended (going up) his pile at 537, and Wealthy ended his pile (going down) on 332, they realized there was something wrong; it took another week to work out what it was.

Colin penned the final number, and said to the expectant Wealthy Vicars, 'That's it then. What next?'

# CHAPTER THIRTEEN

'Unlucky for some.'

'What next? I suggest you wake up and take over from me, that's what next, young Colin.'

Colin looked at the snotty bespectacled oik of about ten sitting next to him at the check-out desk of the library.

'Who are you?'

'Oh, Colin, you are funny. It's me, Brian! If anyone can Brian can.' Snort.

Brian turned and took the next book to be stamped. It was the 1990 World Cup Annual.

'Oh, no, not football again!' he said, and then seemed to play an imaginary clarinet. The youth taking the book out stabbed Brian in the eye with his finger and moved off.

'Thank you, Mr Benton' called Brian, a moronic grin on his face.

As Brian convulsed to the playing of his imaginary clarinet, Colin got up and started to rush out of the library.

'Hoi!' shouted Brian, 'where're you going? It's your shift!' He turned to the next borrower at the desk.

'Sorry about that, Mr Wells.' He leaned closer. 'I think he must have had an accident . . . smelt quite badly, as it happens, though I'm not the one to say anything, of course . . . oof! Thank you, Mr Wells, have a nice day.'

As Brian's shout echoed around the library and the gentle hisses of other staff floated back to the desk, Colin was leaping down the stairs. His mind raced. All those months . . . years that he had been away had been condensed into a few seconds. He wondered whether his body had actually stayed in the chair . . . no, no, he'd have noticed it on the way out with Krap . . . a knife metaphorically pierced his heart at the thought of his fallen hero. He hadn't thought about the great man over the last few months except as a character in a book.

As he ran down the street, Colin remembered the state of his clothing as much from the stares of passers-by as the feel of the urine stiffened legs of his trousers. He slowed to an embarrassed shuffle, then broke into a run again. Past the building societies, Littlewoods, the furniture shop, he ran. The fountain was still there . . . and the bus station. Across the car park he ran, over the road to the steps of his house. He slammed into the front door and only then remembered to turn the handle. (It flashed across his mind that all Threan doors were handle-less or non-existent. Funny he'd never really noticed it in the year . . . days . . . oh bugger it.) He fell into the hallway.

'Colin!' his mother shouted in surprise, then collected herself. 'Is that you?'

She reached out and hugged Colin to her formidable bosom.

'Oh, Colin,' she simpered, 'Mummy's baby got

into trouble den? Come tell mummy. Were you frightened? Yes, I can smell that you jolly well were. What
did they do? Take your money? Dose nasty muggers
take Col-col's money den? Oh, dum dum wa goo
kookoo.'

Colin hated it when his mother was like this. He
was, after all, twenty-one years old now, and just about
to start shaving. Colin's mother, however, was six feet
tall, about fourteen stone and if she decided that her
little boy was going to stay close to her forever, forsak-
ing all others, then that was the way it was going to be.
Her long, grey hair, smelling ever so slightly of chip
fat, covered Colin's face as she dragged him into the
house.

'Ey opp! Sat that little booger down,' boomed his
father. 'Whey's tha bin, lad?'

'Oh, leave the poor lamb alone, will you? He's been
mugged! And he was ever so frightened! Now, off you
go to the bathroom and get cleaned up. We'll talk later.
And you . . .' she turned and shouted at her six foot
two inch, twenty-stone husband who stood at the sink
drying dishes on his pinafore, 'cut that bloody
Yorkshire rubbish out! I've told you before.'

As Colin lay soaking in the bath, he thought that it
really was little wonder that he was as he was. The
house where he had been born (the original stain was
still on the carpet where the placenta had caught his
father by surprise by just flopping out onto the floor)
was no bigger than the library's reference section. No
wonder he needed to escape to the FOCS every week.
He'd go crazy without it, he decided. His chest swelled
(and so did his . . . never mind) as he thought of FOCS.
What stories he had for them. He would relate all the
adventures and stun the lot of them. They'd all be so

impressed, especially Susan . . . he stopped and performed the now well practised swallow-dive from the peaks of hope and excitement to the rock hard trough of despondency.

Susan!

But, of course, she was dead. Returned to Threa to die. And he'd eaten her. His stomach cramped and he swallowed hard on the rising tide. He tried to cut it out of his mind. The water got colder. His brain settled and his eyes closed. He breathed deeply and took little notice of his mother barging in with a towel the size of a dish cloth for him to dry himself on. He was home!

As the days passed, Colin slipped slowly, but surely into the routine of his old life. His job was somehow duller than before (and altogether more horrible with the arrival of the thick-as-a-Tharg's skin Brian, who couldn't take a hint such as 'bugger off' to know when he wasn't wanted) but there was a certain stability to it that reassured him.

His adventures had changed him, no doubt about that. He was now the one called in to collect fines for overdue books and at home he even once refused to eat his greens. His mother despaired; his father quietly welcomed the subtle changes that had taken place. Then came the first FOCS meeting since his return. Saturday night was role-play night in Clacton for the Friends of the Conqueror Society. The members met in a room at the Grammar School. Colin arrived full of anticipation.

Excitement gripped him again as he stripped off his trench coat.

'What have you come as?' asked a girl between chews of her gum. Colin recognized her now as being called Norma. She had only been with FOCS for about two months. The slave girl outfit showed her ample if not a little too ample figure off perfectly. Colin's loins stirred, but he knew there would be time for that later. He looked at Norma challengingly and said, chest puffed out, 'Spasmo!'

'Who's he, an undertaker?' she asked, not really interested. 'I've never heard of him. Why all the black?'

He brushed past her, not deigning to answer this mere mortal, feeling a mile high. There was someone dressed as Krap (Ha! wait till I tell you, you . . . you . . . you git), two people in the same coat as a Tharg (Maybe I'll eat them later), half a dozen slave girls (Not a patch, not a patch, he thought).

There was a 'Mythical Mickey Thom', which allowed you to dress as you liked because there was no description of him in the Chronicles. This one wore jeans and a Status Quo jacket. Two Andrew the Spinelesses with their heads pathetically stuck to their shoulders and a Nels of the Paulon in a G-string and silver gloves completed the gathering. They all stopped talking and looked at him.

'Blimey! Colin! Who's dead?' said Krap exaggeratedly. (Mr Isaac Hunt, thought Colin. You wait!)

'I,' announced Colin loudly, 'am Spasmo. Also known to you poor Earthlings as Lessdick Siding with the Fives, or Spider, Keeper of the Records!'

There was silence as the final echo of his voice died away amongst the wooden benches.

'But how can Lessdick, who was a . . . a . . . and, or Spider the er . . . er oh, OK!' stuttered Nels. Colin was jubilant. To introduce a new characterization was good enough, but to have it so easily accepted was sweet victory indeed. Then he played his ace.

'I'm from *The Chronicles of Ancient Threa*. Or should I

say *The Chronicles of Threa, Ancient and Modern, part Four!*' he announced grandly.

Mickey Thom started to say that they were all from the Chronicles, when he stopped.

'Volume Four? Part four? What are you talking about?' he complained. 'Everyone knows that there's only three parts!'

Jeers and boos were aimed at Colin, and general conversation resumed. Colin started to feel annoyed. This was not going to plan.

'Where's Susan? She'll tell you!' he blurted out without really thinking of what he was saying.

'You bastard!' snarled a plump slave girl as the chat subsided again.

'You know she ran away from her Bob. You callous bastard!'

'Oh, yes, I remember, I ate her,' mused Colin before he realized the impact of his words.

'So it was you,' snapped Krap. 'You were the reason for her breaking up with Bob! Where is she? Where'd she go?' There was a definite menace there, and everyone started to get to their feet.

'No, no, you don't understand, she's dead. It's OK, she was dead when we . . .' Colin stuttered to a halt. He felt the panic welling up inside. The whole group were on their feet now, closing in on him.

'You bastard!' said Krap.

'You . . . you . . . you bastard!' said Nels.

'Why, you bastard!' said the slave girl.

The insults came thick, fast, and threateningly. Colin backed away and hit the wall.

'No, no, please, you don't understand!' he whimpered. Think! he shouted to himself, Think! 'No, I don't mean she's dead at all, I mean, er . . . oh!'

### SUSAN THE SOCIAL WORKER (II)
#### (or 'the joys of spring')
*This is Colin's recollection of Susan on meeting her after his apparent consumption of her dead body. Notice the magical glint in her eyes, the glistening of her teeth, the fullness of her lips and the glowing, healthy vitality in her face. There are no potatoes or vertebrae in this drawing as the mood has shifted to life and fulfilment. These aspects are captured by the bunch of flowers drawn bottom right*

135

Colin was struck dumb. He swallowed hard, but his throat had contracted with fear. The phlegm first choked him, then he had to spit.

Colin stopped in mid-sentence and stared open-mouthed at the doorway. Everyone else stopped talking and turned to look.

Susan stood in the doorway.

At least . . . it *looked* like Susan, but . . . Colin couldn't quite put his finger on it but there was something . . . well . . . different, he fancied. Her hair seemed sort of shinier. She was . . . well . . . sort of bustier, and she had a sparkle in her eye. But it was definitely Susan.

Totally ignoring Colin, she walked over to the others and the throng closed in around her, suddenly animated and noisy once more. The women patted her comfortingly on the shoulders and cooed about how it was such a good, strong act to have left that drunkard Bob and of course she needed time to herself to come to terms with the situation. The men tried to figure out what it was about her that gave off such an aura of . . . well . . . sexiness.

Colin pushed his way through the crowd with a determined look on his face and confronted Susan. The hubbub of conversation died once more as everyone looked at him. 'Um . . . ' he started. 'Ah, I see you're um OK then er Susan,' he mumbled.

Colin thought there was a flicker of recognition in her eyes before she stared straight through him and then, eyes sparkling more fiercely than before, turned back to Krap and continued her conversation as if Colin had never existed. The group closed up around her and Colin was shut out once more.

He didn't remember getting home that night. His mind was in such turmoil. He *had* eaten Susan, he had.

He'd gutted her with loving care and carefully cut strips of flesh off her and cooked her and yet there she was as large as life and breathing and positively glowing. And yet . . . and yet there was something different.

Sleep didn't come easily that night. Colin's brain worked overtime in ever-decreasing circles until he just couldn't think any more.

His dreams were strange and troubled. He was back in the room at the FOCS meeting, wearing a simulated suede thong, and nothing else. He was looking at Susan, her heaving breasts, those bags of fun he had barbecued all those moons ago. He was all a-quiver. The throng patted Susan and his thong gained a life force of its own. The men played pocket billiards and he pulled back his under apparel, revealing a cue of his own. There was something about this new Susan that was blowing the whole room up out of all proportion.

'God, I wouldn't pat her on the shoulders, I'd . . .' he thought out aloud to himself. The rest stared at Colin for a second . . . then the scene dissolved into a silhouette of a topless go-go dancer (how do I know she's topless? thought Colin).

Colin woke with a blinding headache.

The next day was Sunday and Colin only just remembered in time that he had said that he would help tidy the library, do some filing, stuff like that ready for the following week's rush. He had come to no conclusion regarding the reappearance of Susan and in his haste to get to the library, forgot all about her.

Brian opened the front door of the library as Colin ran up breathlessly.

'Hullo, Colin,' he whined. 'Always in a rush, har-har, snort.'

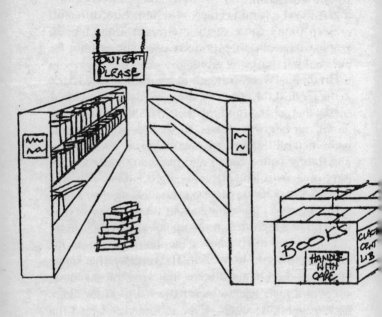

### LIBRARY PICTURES
*Unfortunately the publishers of this tome have decided that the pictures drawn by Colin during his stay on Threa depicting the library where he works were rather too surreal for publication. So we have had to use library pictures as above. Note the life and movement created by the partly stacked shelves and the hoards of books awaiting stacking*

Colin mumbled his way past and went in to put his jacket in the storeroom. Brian followed him and handed him a magazine.

'This was left yesterday in the library. Not one of ours so I thought it could be yours. You are into all that extra-territorial stuff aren't you? Still at least it's not football again, shoop-snort.' He left the room hunched over his imaginary clarinet, fingers working furiously.

Colin glanced briefly at the title and went to put down the rather bulky magazine. He did a double take. It was called *Parallel Universes Weekly* and declared on the front cover it was: 'Simultaneously published weekly in 759 parallel Universes by the Parallel Universe Society'. This was followed by a long list of prices of all types of currencies: two pounds sterling, four thousand lire, twenty spondu, three goats, five goonbellies and so on. Colin had never seen this magazine before and felt a tingle run down his spine. He sat back thoughtfully on the edge of the desk, slipped off and had to pick himself up off the floor. Steadied now, he sat back thoughtfully and read the index inside the front cover.

'In this week's edition:

Why people in the ninth Parallel are nicer than they are in the twenty-seventh . . . *page* 3

What to do if you die in Parallel Universe . . . *page* 5

Are YOU dead in a Parallel Universe? See our easy to use inquiry system . . . *page* 8

Can you move from one Parallel Universe to another? We say YES and show you how it can be done . . . *page* 11

'Can I get rid of my Aura?' Your questions answered on *page* 15.

A strange and preposterous idea started to form in Colin's mind. It involved Susan . . . the difference . . . this magazine . . . Then as he wrestled with the notion coming to him, Colin gasped at the next section.

'Our special Ecological Feature this week covers Environmental problems on the planet Threa. Turn to *page* 18.'

Colin quickly did so, absolutely stunned to see an article about the fabulous, mythical world he had so recently visited. He started to read.

'Our special correspondent, Twad Veanos who, as regular readers will know, is alive in all 759 Universes that *P.U.* publications appear in, reports from Threa, a planet on the brink of ecological disaster. Or is it? Over to you Twad.'

Colin read on avidly.

'Hullo, readers. Well what's new – in fact on Parallel Universe 325 the horseless buggy is quite a recent innovation, but that's not all, my old onion bhajis – it's amazing but all those carbon-base life forms on Threa across all parallel universes are intent on bringing Threa to final damnation.

'As I said in last month's edition of *Parallel Universe Weekly* dated next Tuesday, it is unreal the effect the alcohol had on those carbon-based life forms. So unreal that it's not happening. I can report that from Parallel Universes one through to 759, the planet Threa is in a rapidly degenerating condition. Large groups of new creations in the animal and bug kingdoms seem to be tailor-made to do nothing but eat vegetation.

'So where is our one and only super human, super hero, superannuation, superlative, super man KEER-RAPP – and I'm not talking about laying the old brown cable, boys and girls – but KEERRAPP the Conqueror?

'What is he doing to stop Threa from going down the one way street with only a flagpole to save it?

'In an unexpected cerebral contact with your correspondent yesterday, someone calling themselves, One of the youth or youthful twins in charge of all that is green and bountiful and plant-like and stuff like that claimed that what was needed was a hero . . . "someone to do his building or bidding" (the contact was very weak) to redress or regress the balance between vegetation and the animal kingdom. It was claimed that a hero had been sent for, and should arrive shortly . . . he is a fabulous Barbarian or Librarian or something by the name of . . .'

Something fell to the floor from inside the magazine. Colin picked it up and stared in horrified fascination. It was a pull-out section entitled, 'the final part of our serialization of *The Chronicles of Ancient Threa* . . . part four. With our thanks to Wealthy Vicars'.

Colin's jaw wouldn't close as he thumbed through the special supplement. He skim-read his adventures the way he had written them. He got to the bit right at the end that said 'And yea, verily, then did Colin return home and soon after suffer a very painful and horrible death,' when the whole magazine was pulled from his grasp and he snapped out of the trance.

'Someone here says this is his magazine, Colin old chap. Have to give it back I'm afraid, eh what?'

Colin slowly followed Brian out of the room, still unable to come to grips with the events of the past few moments. He saw Brian give the magazine at the far end of the library to an absolute giant of a man; seven feet tall he must be, thought Colin . . . and and as broad, and wearing a blue pin-striped suit and *wire rimmed glasses* with *long dark hair* and and . . . *a broadsword protruding below the bottom of his side-vented jacket.*

The man looked straight through Colin without a hint of recognition, then turned and disappeared into the street. Colin stood frozen to the spot.

'Krap!' he gasped out aloud.